ADVENTURE
IN
ANCIENT AZORKA

TIME RIDER

CORRIE GILMOUR

ISBN 978-1-967361-05-2 (Paperback)
ISBN 978-1-967361-06-9 (Ebook)

Inquiries and Book Orders should be addressed to:

Leavitt Peak Press
17901 Pioneer Blvd Ste L #298, Artesia, California 90701
Phone #: 2092191548

SPECIAL THANKS AND APPRECIATION

Corrie Gilmour, the author, provided the artwork that was to dark and still needed work. Jessica Bailey finished the cover and did a spectacular job. Many thanks to Jessica Bailey.

DEDICATION

I dedicate this book to all the courageous individuals who stood against the tyranny of the Nazis, including the brave German people who resisted from within. Your sacrifices and acts of defiance, both great and small, are an enduring testament to the strength of the human spirit and the unwavering pursuit of justice. This book is also a tribute to the memory of the Holocaust, a solemn reminder of the atrocities faced by millions, and a call to ensure that such horrors are never forgotten nor repeated.

TABLE OF CONTENTS

CHAPTER 1

Magdeburg, Germany---November 14th 1944

Black clouds advanced across a winter sky, almost dark, the last of the deep red clouds sinking in the distance. The full moon shone bright and looked down on the approaching vehicle.

Captain Gunther Bohm was thinking ahead as he sat in the back of a 1943 twelve-cylinder black limousine which was now racing uphill on this winding road. The limousine's headlamps shone on the black helmet of an SS guard standing at attention on the side of the road. Gunther held his right arm up, saluting him. Access to this road was restricted and the SS had provided guards for this meeting every one-hundred yards all the way to the top of the hill. The road will stop in front of a nineteenth-century estate, now occupied by Major Wilhelm, the officer in charge of special operations for Germany's air force, the Luftwaffe. They will park, then Gunther will meet his commander's guests, a special moment he had been waiting for since leaving Berlin two hours ago with his orders and mission details.

The captain casually glanced out the front windshield and saw the shadows of November elms which lined both sides of the narrow road, dancing on the polished and gleaming surface of the black limousine's hood. The lower branches of the trees held a layer of snow while the top branches reached out to the sky, narrow and skeletal, moving about as though warning of the coming storm.

Despite the damp chill, Gunther had to wipe away the perspiration trickling down from his thick brown hair. He looked at his watch. It was five-thirty and he was on time. He watched his corporal, a skilled driver, handling the limousine through the turns in the road.

"Fritz, how much further do we have to travel before we arrive." Gunther asked. His dark brows seemed to arch downwards as though anticipating a disappointing response.

Fritz turned his head quickly, a lock of his blonde hair fell down on his forehead, covering an inch-long scar above his right eye.

"Another five minutes and we'll be there, sir."

Fritz turned back around, looking ahead to a steep hill they were nearing. The captain remained silent, returning to his thoughts about the mission. He had been briefed about three special ladies from "Ubersinnlich Forschungs". He would be working with them on behalf of the "Ahnenerbe" organization which was established in response to the leadership's quest for ancient relics which some believed would help win the war.

Ancient technology harbored lost advancements which could be advantageous in war. In some cases, there was a wealth of information left behind in the pyramids. Some of this information, when properly translated, suggested different types of energy could be used in place of oil for home heating and gasoline for military vehicles.

Gunther knew this mission would not be as straight forward as securing relics and papyrus records from the "City of the Dead". That mission almost got Fritz killed. Fortunately, he dodged the Arab's bullet but it still nicked him leaving the ugly scar above his eye. The new mission will be ice cold temperatures instead of the blistering heat of the desert. It will be a coordinated effort with the UF/Gesellschaft ladies in order to secure information which the leadership requires. Cheer up Fritz, Gunther thought, this will be a mission you'll enjoy.

While a wicked smile creased Gunther's fifty-year old, weather-beaten face, he continued to be lost in his thoughts. Up ahead the road was ending, and they were only one-hundred-yards from the mansion's circular driveway. As they approached, Fritz could see bright light pouring out from a large window on the upper floor, where a room had been converted into an office by the Nazis. The window was flanked by two dormer-style windows on each side which were shuttered. The lower floor, its large windows now dark, was constructed with fieldstone and hand carved pillars, painted white, that ran the length of the porch. The upper level walls were finished in white stucco and dark wood. The roof was shingled in dark wood and red brick was used for the chimney.

Inside the upper office of the ten-thousand square-foot mansion, three of the "Third Reich's" finest soldiers, and members of the UF society, stood silently at attention in front of Major Wilhelm. The major was five-foot-nine, broad shouldered with an athletic build. He was comfortably seated at his mahogany desk, dressed in a white shirt with black tie, his shiny swastika cufflinks occasionally reflecting the overhead lamp beside him. The major faced the office window and looked outside briefly. He leaned back in his leather chair and picked up a document with the seal of the 'Third Reich' in the top right corner. Brushing his thick red hair back with his hand, he began reading the document. A few more moments of silence followed before he looked up from the paper and addressed the young ladies standing at attention in the office.

Ingrid Thomamuller, Hilda Friedland and Helga Bjorling were highly trained soldiers with special skills and abilities. Their offensive and defensive hand-to-hand combat techniques have been enhanced with martial arts training. They were captains and accomplished marks-women and had won many competitions for target shooting. Special classroom study sessions had sharpened their intellectual abilities which they used now, listening carefully to their commander.

"Ingrid, Hilda, and Helga, it is my pleasure to brief you on your mission." Major Wilhelm began.

"As you already know, in 1938 we sent a team of scientists, explorers, military units and building crews to the 'Queen Maude' region of Antarctica. Whaling ships and submarines carried our personnel without attracting the attention of our enemies. Our explorers discovered a vast network of underground warm water rivers and caves. The most interesting discovery was a cave that extended down almost three miles from the surface to a large geothermal lake."

He glanced at the ladies with his penetrating blue eyes, waiting to see if they had a comment or question. They stood there silently waiting for him to continue. Outside a deep rumble of thunder roared across the land.

"Now if I'm correct, your classroom studies taught you that volcanoes of the central Atlantic lie along a rift in the earth's crust between two tectonic plates. These tectonic plates are known as the 'South American Plate' and the 'African Plate'. We call this the median rift zone of the 'Mid-Atlantic' ridge.

"The power that we're utilizing is from volcanic activity, which gives us steam and electricity. Construction teams were sent here, and we built a city-sized base which we now call New Berlin. It is also referred to as Base 211."

Major Wilhelm paused to take a drink of water which lay close by on his desk, then continued with the briefing.

"All this effort is a direct result of the 1936 recovery of a crashed disc, our Schutzstaffel made in Freiburg. What we have learned in New Berlin in the last six years is incredible. Now our base hosts the Schutzstaffel, the Thule Society, and the UF Society."

Major Wilhelm stopped talking then looked directly at Ingrid. Like Hilda and Helga, Ingrid was motionless and still at attention.

All three ladies were dressed in formal uniform; pressed black pants and a white shirt with a black tie. Their athletic training has resulted in an average weight of one-hundred and forty pounds. Long blonde hair which draped down their backs was captured in a golden clip so that it would not be a hindrance in combat.

"At ease, ladies." The major held out his right hand, his gesture indicating that they should relax.

All three ladies were close to six-feet tall, athletically built and attractive. But, Ingrid's beautiful heart-shaped face, full red lips, and large blue eyes belie her true nature.

"Ingrid, as you know, Carl has said many interesting things about your combat abilities. He is a close confident of our Fuehrer and Mr. Koszenburg. Carl is very impressed with your skills. This prominent member of your society has also assessed Helga for her unusual communications talent, and of course, Hilda for her natural proficiency with the Luftwaffe's modern aircraft."

The major smiled as he looked at Hilda, who had adopted a more relaxed posture but was completely emotionless as she was usually when praise was about to be heaped upon her.

"Germany thanks you for that 'dog fight' over Britain last month, Hilda. Your Messerschmitt shot down three British Spitfires while you were returning from your bombing mission. The Luftwaffe's command is buzzing with the story. German pride and morale have returned to our air force."

Hilda gave her head a quick nod in acknowledgment. The major was attracted to her beautiful oval face with its girlish dimples and healthy golden skin. However, her almond-shaped deep blue eyes were expressionless, almost cold.

"I thank you, sir. As you must know, it was my absolute pleasure to join that mission. It got me out into the action and the practice keeps my reflexes sharp." Hilda replied. Her voice was melodious, like an opera singer.

Last, but not least, the major thought, was Helga, whose communications talent was almost as powerful as the leader and founder of the UF/Gesellschaft.

"The Reichsmarschall would like to thank you, Helga, for your intel which stopped the Allies' attempted bombing raid on Stuttgart. The 'Fuehrerball' our unmanned interceptor disc, was launched in response. And was responsible for shutting down the plane's engines and causing one-hundred and fifty of them to crash. As you know, our defensive weapon burns chemicals around the ring of the disc to create an electrostatic field which disables bomber engines and radar."

The major thought Helga was beautiful like the other two ladies, but more mysterious. Her grey-blue eyes were piercing and could be very expressive, sometimes malevolent, which is probably why she had earned the reputation 'Nachthexen', night witch. The major looked up at the light outside crossing the window and knew that his other guests had arrived.

"One moment, ladies. I think we've got company."

The major got up from his desk. His black pants were tucked into knee-length black boots which echoed in the room with every footfall on the polished wooden floor. He rushed to the opposite wall and peered out through the window. The three ladies were standing beside him.

"Wonderful! Gunther and Fritz have arrived!" He barked excitedly.

Ingrid, Helga, and Hilda turned to watch the gleeful Major Wilhelm. They thought he was an efficient commander. Yet, wondering if he might get caught off guard someday by being too social.

Gunther and Fritz had been introduced to Major Wilhelm in Salzburg eight years ago and all three had gone out; a night in the town. The major had a fantastic time and got to know more about the important work these two men were involved with. He had selected them for this mission because of their extensive experience with the 'Ahnenerbe' missions.

The major looked down at the circular driveway as Fritz was opening the door for Gunther. Hilda was close to the window and the major. She saw a frown of disbelief suddenly appear on his face. Before she could ask him, what was wrong, a loud gunshot broke the silence.

Outside, the major had seen a fight break out on the far perimeter by the brick fence directly across from his window. One of his men had caught an intruder trying to sneak up on him. There was a struggle but the intruder had overpowered the guard and stabbed him. Unfortunately, when the intruder realized the fight had caught the attention of Fritz, he reached for his rifle, lying on the ground, and fired, shooting Fritz in the head before he could free his 'Luger' pistol from its holster.

Major Wilhelm was raging mad as he reached for his own Luger. He broke a pane of glass from the window and nearly emptied the pistol's magazine in the direction of the enemy intruder hunching down for cover behind the fallen guard. Two more invading companions returned fire, shattering three more window panes close to the surprised major, forcing him to duck for cover.

The major looked over at Helga standing between Hilda and Ingrid. She had closed her eyes, and the major thought, seemed to be concentrating on something. He watched as she leaned her head closer to Ingrid and began whispering in her ear. Ingrid was close to the office door which led out to a landing and twenty-five stairs arranged in a semi-circular staircase which ended on a highly polished marble-floored foyer and front entrance.

"Ingrid." She whispered. "There are two intruders outside ducking down behind the brick fence. We need your help. I can see them, and they have explosives."

Helga whispered urgently but just loud enough for the major to overhear. How could Helga see and know this, the major thought. He was perplexed by the ladies' strange behavior.

Helga's talent was activated by stressful situations automatically. It would turn on and off without her control when in self-defense mode. The experimental injections these three ladies had received in 1942 from the 'Super Soldier Project', had granted each of them different talents. All three were willing to risk their lives on the experiment and were glad they did.

The major watched Ingrid kick off her shoes, pull loose her black tie and burst through the office door falling on her knees and hands on the wooden landing outside the office. He moved closer to the office door.

"Major, please wait in the office while Ingrid completes her mission." Helga shouted.

The major stopped at the office entrance and watched the transformation. Ingrid shrieked in pain once then, ten seconds later, growled. The mansion was dimly lit, but he could still see Ingrid's black socks and pants tearing loose from her body as her proportions doubled in size and the coarse blonde hair of a beast covered her legs and feet which had taken on the appearance of a wolf. Dainty red lips changed into thin black lips surrounded by coarse blonde hair and her mouth expanded with a hideous cracking of bones into jaws with long needle-sharp fangs. A dainty retroussé nose was replaced by a protruding snout and above this abominable feature her beautiful blue eyes had become red as burning coals.

The major was paralyzed with horror. Ingrid stood upright, clenched enormous hands with long claws into fists and howled fiercely, causing the fine artworks mounted on the whitewashed walls to shake. A fearful shriek of wild rage echoed throughout the mansion. The transformation had taken sixty-seconds.

Ingrid left the landing, bounding down the stairs two at a time on all fours. Landing and skidding on the marble-floored foyer below. She reached out for the door with long powerful arms. Her enormous hands with their lethal claws closed on the door knob and Ingrid yanked open the door. The mansion shook as she crashed into the door jamb on the way out into the night to satisfy her bloodlust.

Behind the brick fence, which faced the front door, another intruder stood up with a stick of dynamite in his right hand. He tossed the dynamite at the limousine, but before the explosive reached its target, Ingrid had sprung up over the car and caught the dynamite, landed on the pavement, and tossed it up seventy-feet into the cold night air. It exploded above the forest which bordered the front and back lawns of the mansion.

The first intruder who murdered Fritz, watched as Ingrid stood upright to her full seven-foot height. She reached down over the brick fence, grabbing the intruder with the dynamite by the throat and yanking him up over the five-foot barrier. Ingrid flung him down on the ground. Since the last thirty-seconds of her transformation, which fueled her rage and bloodlust for a fresh kill, Ingrid had been waiting for this moment. She placed her elongated feet, which had grown thick tufts of hair and powerful long claws, on the intruder's thighs, causing him to scream. Then bending down close to him, she saw his pale complexion and fear in his wide-eyed expression. His eyes revolved helplessly. The last thing he saw was Ingrid's enormous jaws opening, revealing a couple rows of large razor-sharp teeth.

While Ingrid's killing had gone on, Major Wilhelm had returned to the window, emptied his Luger of ammunition, and replaced it with a machine gun he found leaning against the corner wall. He was holding down the first intruder and shooting at others who were using the brick wall as cover in various places. Fortunately, reinforcements were arriving down the road and below the hill behind the mansion.

Fritz had left the limousine's headlamps on, which helped to illuminate the scene below. The major watched in horror and disbelief as the beast got up from the dead intruder and pounced on top of the next intruder. He was so afraid of Ingrid that he abandoned his cover behind the dead soldier, shielding him from the major's bullets, to flee. But he had jumped up too late to escape Ingrid. His screams o terror and pain echoed around the parking area below. The major watched as a powerful arm covered in blonde fur and outfitted with long claws on a huge hand, sliced through the air, suddenly cutting off the intruder's shrieks.

The major shook himself free from his amazement and carried or with his machine gun. He happened to notice that Helga was smiling coldly, still standing in place beside Hilda. The major killed two more intruders who were trying to escape by edging their way around to the back of the mansion. Then he focused his attention on Ingrid.

The beast Ingrid had become, stood upright again and sniffed the air. She craned her neck in the direction of two more intruders who were fleeing into the woods and down the hill. There was a crackling of branches, and she could hear their footfalls as they frantically fled down the hill.

The threat of invasion had passed, and the chaotic scene calmed down. Ingrid turned to look up at Major Wilhelm, who was still shocked by all he had witnessed. He would be replaying the gruesome events of the night over and over again in his mind until the day he died.

Major Wilhelm was finding what he had seen difficult to believe. That such a dainty and petite lady could turn into a raging beast so rapidly- But not only that, she had enough intelligence to catch the dynamite and throw it high into the air, removing the threat from the surrounding soldiers.

The beast began to shrink in height. Coarse blonde fur was replaced by twenty-five-year old skin on the naked body of a beautiful blonde native of Germany.

There were a few bullets on the driveway pavement around Ingrid's naked feet that had popped out of her body after returning to human form. She looked up to the office, noticing that the major, no longer standing at the window, had respectfully withdrawn himself from gazing at her naked body. She knew that Hilda or Helga would come out with a blanket to cover her, and she didn't want to move until they did. Soldiers were running in every direction checking to be sure there was no longer a threat from more attacks. They were also searching for evidence that would help them discover who the attackers were.

It was cold and wet with a brisk wind sweeping rain across the driveway. Ingrid's hair had begun to stick to her skin and she was shivering. Finally, Hilda walked through the open front door with a large grey blanket in her hands and rushed over to Ingrid. She wrapped the large blanket around Ingrid's shoulders. Hilda was an inch taller and looked like a big sister guiding Ingrid back into the mansion with her arm around her shoulders.

A couple of SS soldiers ran past them on the driveway and entered the mansion, rushing upstairs to report to Major Wilhelm.

The major, sitting at his desk and talking to Helga, heard the footfalls on the staircase, and he turned to face the office door. One soldier remained on the landing and the corporal rushed in, stood at attention, and saluted.

"Sir, while searching outside, we found this notebook in the pocket of a dead intruder. It is written in Russian." The corporal said, practically out of breath from his exertions.

The major took the notebook from the corporal and examined the writing under the lamp beside his desk. Helga remained standing in place watching the major's quizzical expressions. She had picked up on a language she couldn't understand during the emergency which triggered her talent. But, of course, she was compelled to concentrate on the danger, not her curiosity. Major Wilhelm raised his bushy red eyebrows in surprise, then looked over to the corporal.

"This is the Russian language, corporal. I assume you don't know how to write or speak in Russian."

"No sir. Sergeant Hans Steger recognized it. He spent a year on the Russian front, so he's familiar with some of the language."

"I see. Corporal, what else have you found that might link this to an attack by Russian spies?"

"We found explosives behind the brick fence, just a short distance from the first intruder. There were three sticks of dynamite wrapped together."

"Corporal, how many enemy agents got away? Do you have an estimate?"

"Sir, I regret to inform you that we believe two enemy agents got away. Sergeant Steger found a couple of our German shepherds, dead from poison, just twenty-yards from the brick fence beside the driveway's entrance."

Major Wilhelm thought a moment, then he asked one more question.

"How were the enemy dressed? Did you notice if their boots were military issue or a standard for civilians?"

"Sir, you make a brilliant point. It is unlikely that they would sacrifice their military boots. I regret we didn't check. I'll organize the inspection, sir. As for your first question, they were dressed as civilians."

Silence followed while Major Wilhelm thought about the orders he would give to the corporal.

"Corporal, I would like Sergeant Steger to contact 'Schutzstaffel'. He will report that we came under attack by a large force of Russian spies, and that two of them got away, and seven of the enemy were killed. Fritz from the 'Ahnenerbe' organization died in the attack, and Captain Gunther Bohm survived. Give a brief description of how the intruders were dressed, our location, and the direction the two escaping agents fled."

"One more thing, corporal. Has Captain Bohm finished with the paper work and arrangements for Fritz."

"I saw him in conversation with our commander, so I would assume he will be finishing up the details by now, sir."

Very good, corporal. That will be all." Major Wilhelm said, then saluted briskly.

The corporal returned the salute then left the room, walking quickly past the ladies who were on their way up the staircase. Everyone in his unit would keep secret what they witnessed while on duty; a necessary security precaution when guarding top secret developments. The corporal considered Ingrid to be in this category and glad she was on their side. However, the petite blonde still scared him to death.

Hilda led the way into the office, her arm around Ingrid who was still recovering from her transformation. It usually takes Ingrid ten minutes to recover and actually feel energized. The transformation rejuvenates the body at a cellular level, it just has a short delay.

Major Wilhelm walked over to Ingrid and noticed what looked like a bullet wound in her neck. It had already started healing. Ingrid was prepared for his question.

"It is painless, major, and the affected area only feels warm."

"In twenty-four hours, it will completely disappear. When I'm shot after I have shape-shifted, the bullet will be stopped by the beast's skin. An unusual and unexpected effect from the experiment that I've come to appreciate."

"Remarkable, Ingrid. How long have you had this..this gift for combat?" The major stumbled.

"I discovered my new ability shortly after participating in the "Super Soldier Project" in 1942. They injected me with a drug that would allow me to shape-shift, which is what I call the transformation, into a wolf. A wolf with extraordinary strength, yet still possessing the intelligence I have in human form."

The major thought for a moment then asked his question.

"What about Helga and Hilda? Do they have super abilities? Is that why the three of you are together?"

"Helga and Hilda received the same injections as me, but they have different abilities. Our commander for the 'Super Soldier Project' has grouped us together for this mission." Ingrid explained.

"We have been together for many years and have trained and entered competitions. As close friends, we can accomplish a great deal and I believe that the project commander understands this. Our new abilities offer the best results for team work." Ingrid concluded.

Major Wilhelm listened attentively. He was amazed at what he had seen, and could now believe some of the rumors he'd heard among Germany's senior officers. The secrecy concerning the ladies' enhanced abilities through the 'Super Soldier Project' left him unprepared for this surprise. The major thought the ladies were well trained combatants and members of UF/Gesellschaft. He wondered why he was not briefed on this. The major had no further questions or comments on the matter and decided to change the subject. Probing further could be regarded as a breach of security.

"Clothing may be found three doors down the hall. The former occupants of this home were forced to leave with just the clothing on their backs. You should be able to find your size Ingrid. The young woman in the house was about five-foot-ten-inches tall and athletic like you. She probably has the same size of clothing you require."

Ingrid thanked the major, leaving the room to find an outfit that would be comfortable and warm.

A couple of minutes later, the same corporal who had left to deliver the sergeant's orders appeared in the doorway.

"Would the major like us to search every room in the mansion?" The corporal asked.

"That won't be necessary so long as we have Helga. She would have picked up the presence of an intruder." The major replied.

"Very good sir." The corporal saluted then turned to leave, albeit with a slight look of confusion on his face.

In the next room, Ivan Artemiev breathed a sigh of relief. It must be the metal plate the doctors in Stalingrad used in the operation on his severely fractured skull. The metal plate is blocking out Helga's ability to detect my presence, he thought. That's why she doesn't know I'm here listening in on their conversations.

A few years ago, Ivan was fighting the German military in Stalingrad. He had been seriously wounded while rescuing two of his comrades. A large chunk of his skull had been affected by an explosion, resulting in severe fracture and some of the bone missing. The commanding officer was impressed with Ivan, and arranged for the best doctors in Russia for his operation. Eventually, the intelligence units stationed in Stalingrad got wind of Ivan's story and reported it to their superiors in Moscow. Moscow offered Ivan a promotion to captain upon the successful completion of his special training. The new captain excelled in the following two missions he was sent on. Moscow headquarters were delighted. They had another mission in mind for Ivan. Ivan's superiors wanted him to kidnap three very special ladies that the Nazis had specially trained.

They reasoned that Germany was low on resources and personnel. Infiltrating enemy territory was getting easier. Now we need to know more about the special projects we discovered. Could those projects affect the final outcome of the war? Russia would interrogate the three ladies and find out.

That's how Ivan found himself standing in a small library closet next door to a Luftwaffe Major and three ladies, two of whom were monsters. He listened through the closet's wall for valuable information, but in the back of his mind he wondered how he would kidnap a werewolf.

Ivan assembled his team in Berlin. Training for his men was intense and lasted two weeks before he felt they were ready. Ivan could speak fluent German and so could Nikolai and Mikhail, although Boris could not. So, Ivan got around this problem by having Boris play the part of a mute. Boris also drove the truck that would hold the three modified coffins the unconscious kidnapped ladies would occupy on their way back to Russia.

The plan was to park the truck at the bottom of the hill facing away from the mansion for their departure. The agents would be able to escape through the backyard then down the hill. Boris would place canvas over the coffins. Then he would open the engine hood so that those passing by on the road would think the truck had engine trouble and the driver was fixing the problem.

The rest of the agents would climb the hill and poison the dogs. Then the agents would find their positions behind the brick wall, waiting for the signal to begin. Ivan would enter the mansion in a German uniform and find the mansion's library without attracting attention.

They had explosives just in case there were more German soldiers than they had expected. Dynamite comes in handy when subduing overwhelming numbers of enemy soldiers.

Still, even with flawless planning, something went wrong. Maybe the limousine pulling in the driveway with its bright headlights exposed one of his men. If all had gone well, the men would eliminate the perimeter guards then enter the mansion, silently creeping up the stairs, rushing the office, killing the major and capturing the ladies. Ivan would join them and administer the knockout drug by injection. They would carry the ladies downhill, place them in the coffins and drive off.

Before the ladies had arrived, Ivan had drilled a small hole in his side of the wall and installed a small listening device. The first shocking bit of information came from a phone call the major received from Luftwaffe headquarters.

The secretary for the supreme commander of the Luftwaffe relayed a message to the major and the major repeated it word for word as he wrote the message down, making Ivan's job even easier. The Reichsmarshall wanted to know about the strategic advantages that Antarctica could offer the Luftwaffe. What kind of runway could they expect and shelter for the aircraft. The British were close by, protecting their own interests in the region. Then the secretary wanted to know if Major Wilhelm had received the new instructions and parts for the modifications to the flying disc they were working on in Cologne. Major Wilhelm had responded by saying the flight from Antarctica hadn't arrived yet, but he would notify headquarters the moment it did. He asked if there were further messages or instructions for him and when confirming there weren't he hung up.

That one phone call answered a lot of questions his superiors would have, Ivan thought, and would also produce new questions. He waited for the ladies to arrive and that's when he got his next surprise. The 'Super Soldier Project' has produced some very interesting results.

But now, Ivan knew he had to make his escape before the perimeter guards had a chance to reorganize their positions. He reached over and quietly pulled the listening device from its place on the wall, wrapped it up, and put it in the pocket of his German uniform. He opened the closet door and stepped out into the darkened room. It was covered wall to wall, with bookshelves, hiding the white walls. Like the stairway spindles, the wood trim around the window was stained dark brown. The floor was teak wood and Ivan had to tread lightly, so his footsteps wouldn't be heard.

He heard footsteps outside in the hall. Maybe it was Ingrid returning from her search for clothing. In a couple of minutes, Ivan heard Ingrid's voice next door in the office, confirming his suspicion. She had returned wearing a black turtle-neck sweater and black ski pants. Ivan walked across an expensive teak floor, past bookcases and almost ran his shins into a coffee table in the middle of the room that shared the space with two leather chairs.

Ivan crept quietly to the back of the room where two French doors led to an outside patio. He opened a door and stepped outside beside a small table and two chairs. He closed the door, walked to the back of the patio and looked over the hand-carved railing. It was only a fifteen-foot drop to the backyard, then a fifty-yard dash across the lawn to the hill at the back of the property.

Ivan was about five-foot ten and one-hundred eighty pounds of solid muscle. He was glad the German builders were so meticulous because not one floor board of the porch squeaked. He carefully climbed over the railing. The shadowy backyard was free of guards for the moment, so he dropped to the ground and ran across the back lawn and down the hill.

Ivan hoped the two men that had escaped would be waiting close by the truck. They had planned this if the mission failed. What Ivan didn't know, is that the two men were spooked when Boris disappeared. They had hidden in the back of a civilian truck parked at the bottom of the hill, which unexpectedly left before they could abandon their hiding spot. The missing Boris had met with a fatal accident, tripping in the dark and landing headfirst on a sharp rock in the ditch.

Ivan reached the truck and saw that Boris was in a ditch, ten-yards from him, face down in the water near the sharp rock he had fallen on. Ivan walked up to the front of the truck and closed the engine's hood, then walked back and got in the driver's seat. He examined himself in the mirror, brushing some dirt out of his blonde crewcut hair. He removed his German uniform, turning it inside out to hide the German insignia. Then he changed into black pants and pulled a brown leather jacket over a navy-blue sweater. He had to look like a driver delivering three empty coffins to a funeral home.

Ivan tossed his German uniform into the ditch then decided to wait a further, nerve-wracking ten minutes, giving his men extra time to return to the rendezvous. They failed to show up, so he drove off.

While Ivan made his escape, back at the mansion, a shaken Captain Bohm arrived in the office.

"Franz. Oh, pardon me, Major Wilhelm, sir." Gunther stammered. He stood at attention saluting the major.

The major returned his salute and said, "You can dispense with the formality, Captain Bohm. I'm very sorry for the loss of Fritz. He will be missed. Our guard lost the struggle with his attacker otherwise Fritz would still be with us."

"Fritz will be missed. He was like a brother to me." Gunther replied.

Gunther ran a handkerchief down his large straight nose, catching a few droplets of rain. His beady, brown eyes were communicating sadness. What he was really thinking wasn't brotherly love. Fritz had taken on the more dangerous tasks during their missions and saved his life more than once. Gunther was afraid of dying to the point of cowardice, but he always had an explanation for his actions.

"I saw Fritz fall after the shot rang out. Then there seemed to be a rain of bullets flying everywhere, so I used my door as cover and joined the fire fight, targeting enemy agents walking towards us from the front entrance. Shortly after, I felt the car and ground tremble as something crossed the driveway.

"I remember during the shooting, I thought I heard a large dog growl. However, my attention was focused on defeating the invaders, so I didn't turn around to satisfy my curiosity." Gunther recalled.

"I'm glad you're safe because you have important work to do with these three charming ladies." The major said.

"Let me introduce you to Helga, Hilda and Ingrid." The major pointed to Helga then Hilda and Ingrid as the three ladies returned a smile.

Gunther smiled and clicked the heels of his polished black boots, and did a quick bow.

Helga was secretive about mind reading, but she caught some of Gunther's thoughts. He was a despicable coward. Afraid of combat is not the quality of soldier we are looking for, she thought. However, he's one of the top archeologists for the 'Ahnenerbe' and we'll have to cover for him. He had better be good at reading those tablets, or maybe we'll feed him to Ingrid for lunch.

At this thought, a quick smile broke out and her beautiful complexion flushed red. She noticed the major had caught her change in expression.

"I'm sorry major. That picture up there on the wall is amusing." Helga pointed to the comical painting behind the major. A group of fat people were seated at a long dining room table, while laughing, drinking and stuffing themselves on roast beef.

The major turned, looked up at the picture and then smiling he clapped his hands.

"That's a great idea! Why don't we go down to the kitchen and have a quick meal before we review your mission? A little something to replenish our energy levels."

The major turned back to his guests and looking at Helga, Hilda and Ingrid, he seemed to be deciding something.

"Lead the way to the kitchen Helga." The major said with a big smile creasing his fifty-year old features.

Helga was sure that the major was testing her to see if she already knew the way to the kitchen through the use of her psychic ability. There was no imminent danger that would cause her ability to turn on and focus. No intruders in the kitchen. She could always read a person's thoughts since the injection from the project, but that was a secret that Helga would not share, not even with the UF Society.

"Major. I actually don't know the way to the kitchen. Perhaps you should lead."

"Very well. Alright everyone, follow me." Major Wilhelm said.

He led the way out of the office and his guests followed him downstairs to the kitchen. On the way down the stairs, the major noticed that during Ingrid's transformation she had not damaged the gilded rail or upset the string of paintings that decorated the landing and stairway walls. He thanked her for being so considerate. He was also wondering about her new ability. How could a raging beast be considerate?

Gunther overheard the major's conversation with the ladies and was puzzled. What were they talking about? Why had the major thought that Helga knew the way to the kitchen?

At the bottom of the staircase they turned left, walked down a short hallway and entered an eight-hundred square foot kitchen. It was fully equipped and tastefully decorated in red tile which ran to a back wall made from brown brick.

Gunther's solemn expression quickly changed to an ear to ear smile. He pulled down a frying pan from a wall where the pots and pans were hung.

"I've been dreaming about ham and eggs all day!" He said.

"Black Forest ham is in the fridge with the eggs." The major piped up.

Gunther walked over to the fridge while the three ladies sat down at a large oak table close to the brick wall and used for informal dining. The three UF ladies had found some cheese and cold cuts, and they added fresh fruit to their plates from a basket on the table.

Major Wilhelm opened the stove door and pulled out a roast which had finished cooking one hour ago. He brought the roast to the table and joined the ladies. He offered them a slice of roast beef but Hilda and Helga politely declined. The major offered Ingrid some roast beef and she accepted. Ingrid took the largest slice of roast beef on the plate. The major could see a droplet of saliva beginning to form on her bottom lip.

"What a wonderful snack, major. I think the excitement made us all a little hungry." Helga suggested with an expression of gratitude.

Ingrid and Hilda were watching Gunther with a peculiar combination of curiosity and disgust. His appetite was too hardy for a person who had suffered the loss of a friend, and he wasn't offering anyone a slice of the ham he had cut. However, they were respectfully masking their feelings knowing they would have to work with him for a certain period of time while on the mission. Under the bright lights of the kitchen, they saw he was overweight and had a 'pot-belly.' He looked more like an academic than a soldier. When he removed his officer's cap, Hilda had expected a big round bald spot, but to her surprise, Gunther had a head full of thick dark brown hair lightly peppered with grey. He had dark skin from his time in Egypt, and he was heavily wrinkled, making him appear closer to sixty years of age instead of fifty.

Maybe, Hilda thought, archeologists age faster from exposure to the sun. Gunther was Germany's hope for deciphering the plates and her heart seemed to sink at that thought. Like her companions, Hilda was very patriotic and loyal. Maybe Gunther is smarter than he looks. Hilda shrugged off her speculation and continued eating her evening snack.

Gunther had finished cooking his eggs and joined the others at the large rectangular oak table. Hilda, he thought, had beautiful eyes which were a deep blue color. Her golden hair was thicker than her two companions. Her nose was elegantly straight and perfectly compatible with her facial features, especially her seductive smile.

Ingrid had thinner blonde hair, a milk white complexion and large round blue eyes. Those eyes were practically luminous and seemed to bore uncomfortably into Gunther's soul as he discreetly observed her. Gunther had missed Ingrid's transformation, and had mistaken the growling sounds outside for a large dog. He noticed her beautiful lips and mouth were slightly wider than her companions. Although she wasn't smiling now that she had caught Gunther's greedy eyes on her.

After thanking his lucky stars for such attractive company, Gunther noticed that Helga wasn't smiling either. She was looking daggers at him. Gunther looked away from those haunting and malevolent piercing blue eyes and returned to shoveling down his food.

The major had been silent throughout the meal. He was thinking back to the earlier days of the 'Third Reich' when he was younger and stronger. Optimism was in the air and on the edge of every conversation in Germany. Back in those days, Franz Wilhelm was an essential member of the leadership. He also worked on the extremely secretive 'Flying Disc Program' which was advancing rapidly thanks to the undamaged drive from the crashed flying disc, of unknown origin, recovered in 1936.

Ten years later, he became a slave to alcohol. Perhaps that contributed to him being left out of the information loop for other highly secretive programs. He had lost the confidence of the leadership who were now in Antarctica.

In any case, that drink was the only thing now that would calm his nerves and he had eaten enough roast beef to soak up a couple of good shots of Schnapps. But before he could relax, he had one more task. The major knew he had a very important phone call to make upstairs from his office and decided to excuse himself.

"Will you please excuse me ladies and Gunther. I have an important call to make. After tonight's calamity, we have to be cautious. I want to see if we can arrange for your departure earlier than scheduled."

He got up from the table, bowed to his guests, then turned, leaving the kitchen. The major walked back through the short hallway and reaching the foyer, he raced up the twenty-five stairs two at a time. He reached the office almost out of breath but just in time to pour himself a couple of shots of his favorite liquor.

The major had to call Schutzstaffel headquarters in Berlin to request the highway be cleared and guarded from Magdeburg to Leipzig. There was an intelligence leak, and he didn't want to take any chances with the route they'd travel for their flight out of Germany. His guests would have to travel at maximum speed to the airfield in Leipzig and leave immediately for Antarctica. So, he picked up the phone and placed his call.

When the major's call was answered from the other end, he practically shouted at the receiver.

"Hello, its Major Wilhelm calling. Is Hintzinger..." He stuttered, catching his mistake.

n the other end, confusion was beginning to rain down in the mind of the captain answering the call.

"Excuse me major, I thought you said Hintzing. Is that correct. I don't think we..."

The major interrupted him before he could finish.

"Is number one free, captain. It's an emergency." He yelled into the phone.

The captain must have been struggling with the phone call because there was still silence on the other end.

The major took a deep breath and calmed himself down.

"I'm Major Franz Wilhelm, in charge of special operations for the Luftwaffe. I have an emergency situation. I need to speak with number one."

"I'm sorry, sir. I didn't catch what you were saying. We have already received communication from Sergeant Steger and dispatched a team to capture the escaping spies. I'll get number one on the line right away." The captain said in his most apologetic tone of voice.

The major waited patiently, satisfied that the captain didn't hear the double's real name. Mr. Hintzinger took six months to locate, but it was worth the wait because he looked just like number one. The next step in the operation was more complicated. A low speed car accident was staged and when the undercover SS agent got to the targeted car, he pretended to be helping the shaken Hintzinger. Instead, he wrapped a cloth soaked in chloroform over the mouth of Mr. Hintzinger causing him to black out. Hintzinger was taken to a private hospital ward, restricted from the public, and for six weeks he was hypnotized and reconditioned to believe he was no longer Mr. Hintzinger. Mr. Hintzinger believed he was number one, Germany's most feared head of Schutzstaffel.

When he was released, he apologized to the Fuehrer for taking so long to recover. Since his release, you couldn't tell him from the real number one, except during moments like this, because the double was not privy to the Antarctica mission.

"Hello Major Wilhelm, I understand that you encountered some Russian spies tonight and that my men have been dispatched to catch the spies that escaped." The double spoke with the voice of the real leader.

"Yes sir, that is correct. I'm sorry for interrupting you, but I need the highway completely clear and guarded from Magdeburg to Leipzig so that my agents are not challenged again. I plan to send them off in another hour for the airfield in Leipzig where a plane is waiting. They are on a very important mission for the Reichsmarschall." Major Wilhelm finished.

"I will see to it that the highway is clear, and I'll post as many guards as we can spare along the way." The double replied.

"Thank you, sir." Major Wilhelm said.

Major Wilhelm hung up the phone, and walked over to the office door. His guests had left the kitchen and were wandering around downstairs looking at the priceless art which hung on the living room wall. He called them to join him in the office and returned to his desk.

Captain Bohm was the first through the door and sat down close to the window on an expensive leather upholstered chair. The three ladies arrived shortly after and took a seat on the leather couch they had been standing in front of before the attack.

Major Wilhelm began with the briefing for their mission.

"When you arrive in Antarctica, a 'Blohm and Voss BV 238 Floatplane' will be in the water close to the west entrance to New Berlin. The east entrance to New Berlin is used by our submarines. I'm sure Hilda is familiar with our giant flying boat which will have delivered eighty of our best troops and more supplies by that time. It is powered by six Daimler-Benz piston engines; three per wing. We have also arranged for a short expedition to the large disc recently discovered by our explorers who brought back the plates. We are relying on your expertise, Gunther, so we believe the short expedition will be of some help to you with your task. A 'Junker Ju 52 trimotor' will be available for the expedition, and I'm sure Hilda is familiar with this plane." The major paused and raised a glass of water to sooth his parched throat.

"I'm familiar with the Junker, major. What will be waiting on the Leipzig airfield?" Hilda asked.

The major set his glass of water back down on the desk continued with the briefing.

"We have a 'Focke-Wulf FW 200' that has been outfitted with two 7.92 mm machine guns and four 13mm guns and one 20mm cannon. The modifications are concealed within the craft and can be accessed by opening the panel for each weapon. We have a pilot and co-pilot from the Luftwaffe so you can rest on the way to Antarctica."

The major paused briefly, waiting to see if there were any questions. There were no questions so he continued.

"Like the Junker and BV 238, all national insignia have been removed from the plane, so it will appear as a commercial airline for civilians. The BV 238 aircraft is considered by our enemies as part of our whaling station. We have to take the necessary precautions against discovery because the British are in this area protecting their land claims and sometimes patrol the area."

The major noticed a frown on Hilda's face. He was sure that she had a question.

"Hilda, do you have a question." He asked.

"Yes major. I remember hearing about an engineering defect in the aft fuselage section of the Folke-Wulf FW 200."

"That has been remedied and repaired, Hilda." The major replied.

"I have no further questions, major. You have prepared well for our needs and have been a perfect host. I thank you." Hilda said.

This compliment helped the major relax. But something in their conversation triggered a brief feeling of nostalgia and a strangely distant look appeared on his face.

"Ladies, how long have we been working together on the UF/ Gesellschaft program?"

Helga answered the major's question.

"We've been together since the crash of the unknown disc in Freiburg. You're one of Germany's top mechanical engineers and your expertise has helped advance the project. Our timely arrival in Antarctica will please the leaders waiting for us, and I'll be sure to mention the efforts of our host."

Helga had stumbled into some of the major's nervous thoughts concerning the war, and felt sorry for him. Like the doubles in place for number one and the Fuehrer, he would be staying behind to face the Russian advance.

Ingrid provided her contribution to the conversation. Like everyone in the room, minus Gunther, she was very patriotic. She wanted to add some positive reinforcement and hope for a commander she had come to admire over the years they had worked together.

"The flying disc program provides the hope for a victorious Germany and the immediate end to the war. Germany will remember your efforts and hard work. major, I would also like to thank you for all your help and I will cherish and remember our relationship until the day I leave this world."

Gunther was more interested in bringing the conversation back to the present time.

"I can't help being curious about those new plates I'll be examining. Are they written in a language or are they using hieroglyphics to communicate their message?"

Major Wilhelm thought about Gunther's question for a moment.

"In total, Gunther, there are twenty platinum plates. My understanding is that some of the language on the platinum plates is unknown and some of the language on other platinum plates is believed to originate from Atlantis. In fact, our experts in New Berlin believe the disc, which is two-hundred and fifty meters in circumference, could be from that civilization's final days. The language on some of the foot-long platinum plates is the same as some of the recovered relics from the pyramids. As you know, Gunther, the Egyptian hieroglyphs identify those relics as gifts from Atlantis."

Gunther's eyebrows rose, a subtle expression of surprise and a reaction that was expected by the major. He had more questions.

"Could these plates simply be instructions concerning the operation of the flying disc, or is it possible we might discover a powerful weapon on board?"

"That's why we're bringing you in on this Gunther. There are ten platinum plates in an unknown language that we need you to translate. The plates we have discovered may help us to weaponize our discs. You have the most experience of all our archeologists in Germany deciphering and reading Atlantean and Egyptian hieroglyphs." The major answered.

"Yes, but if the plates turn out to be operational instructions for the craft, who would be able to fly the disc?" Gunther replied.

"Think positive, Captain Bohm. We haven't had a chance to introduce some of our special talents." Hilda said as she looked at Gunther with a reassuring smile.

Helga thought she might be able to relieve some of Gunther's anxiety. "We'll give you a full explanation concerning our abilities and special talents on the way to the airfield after our briefing with the major." Ingrid was enjoying the discussion. Gunther caught a slight smile appearing on her face. She was relaxed sitting with her legs crossed on the couch in her new all black outfit. In the dim light of the office she looked like a full moon smiling back at him.

"Gunther, in 1937 our society was asked by the Fuehrer to use our psychic abilities to reach out for answers and understanding with regard to the crashed disc discovered in 1936. We didn't have to leave Germany to do this. We used our special abilities to locate the platinum plates and directed our experts to the exact spot for recovery.

"Some of these plates were written in different languages. Inside the disc were technical devices and instructions written on seven of the foot-long platinum plates that helped advance our projects in Berlin and Cologne. Including instructions on how to build the UF-Disc spacecraft. The platinum plates were left behind by an advanced race. A few of these plates recorded the story of our ancestors and all their deeds on our planet. A future timeline is revealed..."

"Hold that thought, Ingrid." Helga interrupted. "We don't have time for this."

Caught that just in time, Helga thought. We have enough challenge with Gunther without adding this revelation.

Gunther looked at each of the three ladies and shrugged his shoulders.

Major Wilhelm got up and walked over to the broken window, and peered outside. All was quiet, and the guards were in place.

"You're in good hands, Gunther. Let these charming ladies explain, as they suggested, on the way to the airfield. But for now, we need to finish the briefing."

He walked back to his desk and sat down. The briefing continued for another hour, and they covered the remaining aspects of their mission, including the unusual ancient buildings they had found in New Berlin.

"Gunther, I know this will be a victorious mission, and I'd like to toast to Germany's success. However, I must consider a security leak and dispatch you fully briefed immediately." Major Wilhelm said.

The ladies got up from the couch and left the office, walking downstairs with Gunther and Major Wilhelm following behind.

Outside, the major leaned close to Hilda and whispered.

"I'll have one of the guards drive you to the Leipzig airfield."

Hilda caught her chance for some fun and quickly spoke up.

"I wouldn't hear of it, major. You've been like family to us all these years, and we want you to be well protected under these circumstances. I can drive us to the airfield."

The major gave a quick nod of approval. Hilda walked over to the driver's door and got in.

Ingrid marched over to the major and gave him a quick hug, then stood back and with a comical grin said, "It has nothing to do with the full moon major, and I can handle silver without it burning me." She giggled mischievously, waved goodbye, and walked over to the limousine opening the rear passenger door and getting in. She sat comfortably in the luxurious leather seat directly behind Hilda and stretched her legs. Lots of room in this limousine and a seat across from me for Gunther she thought.

Gunther shook the major's hand and saluted him. He turned and started walking towards the car, then stopped suddenly and turned back to the major.

"We will have this mission wrapped up in no time. How about we go out on the town when I get back. I mean have a fun time in Berlin." Gunther suggested.

"Gunther, you've got yourself a date." The major laughed.

Gunther turned back and continued walking over to the limousine, getting in the rear passenger door and sitting across from Ingrid.

Helga was last to leave. Like Ingrid, she gave the major a hug.

"Hilda spoke for all of us, major. We've been together a long time. I hope you'll travel west if we are not flying over Germany by January."

Helga reached into her grey coat's pocket and pulled out a sealed scroll of paper and handed it to the major.

"These are orders from the Reichsmarschall. We discussed a final cleansing of the project in Berlin. He's a very thorough officer and doesn't like to leave anything for the enemy. General Zard will handle the disappearance of three-hundred scientists and engineers who were working on the UF Disc spacecraft."

The major put the scroll into his jacket pocket.

"After the cleansing, General Zard will leave Germany in a Luftwaffe jet, joining us in New Berlin. After you've delivered this order on behalf of the Reichsmarschall, you are to join him in Cologne." Helga finished.

"Take care, Helga and don't worry about me."

"I look forward to your return and Germany's swift victory." The major said.

He looked up at the sky as the clouds were breaking up, leaving patches of clear night sky sparkling with stars.

"At least it stopped raining." He turned and walked back into the mansion.

Helga joined the others, positioning herself in the front seat beside Hilda, who turned the ignition key as soon as she had settled in. The twelve-cylinder limousine roared its approval of Hilda, leaving a plume of smoke behind to slowly dissipate over the rain-soaked driveway.

Hilda drove down the hill slowly so that they could salute the SS guards stationed along the way. Halfway down the hill, Ingrid hung out the window and yelled, "Victory for Germany my brothers." This got her a salute, smile, and sometimes a chuckle.

At the bottom of the hill, Hilda swung the limousine onto the highway to Leipzig, and accelerated to ninety-kilometers per hour. Helga turned around in the front passenger seat and faced Gunther.

"I'm sure you've heard, Gunther, about the 'Third Reich's Super Soldier Project'. The three of us are in the program and have received the injection which has granted us some very special abilities."

Gunther realized this discussion was going to be an orientation, but he had a puzzled look on his face, not knowing what to expect.

"Yes, I've heard of the program but wasn't aware of its progress."

"It has been very successful, Gunther, and as a result, I am able to meditate with greater precision than I did before, which is how I helped the Luftwaffe stop an enemy air raid. I have another talent that turns on automatically if we're in danger. I can locate and identify the threat in great detail, so we can avoid it or destroy it before it strikes."

"Would you have other telepathic talents, Helga?" Gunther asked.

Helga was surprised by Gunther's question, maybe a little unsettled because he was fishing for mind reading. But then she would simply deny the ability.

"No Gunther, I have no other talents. Hilda has telekinetic powers. She can manipulate objects with her mind, causing them to rise and move swiftly. And last but not least, Ingrid is a shape-shifter. What you thought was a dog growling tonight was actually Ingrid."

Ingrid looked across to Gunther with her girlish smile and giggle. She reassured him.

"You're in good paws...I mean hands Gunther. And don't worry, I've been fed."

Ingrid's sense of humor was rewarded with a smirk from Helga and a chuckle from Hilda sitting beside her.

Helga fixed her piercing blue eyes on Gunther.

"Remember, if I don't warn you of danger, you're safe. So, relax and enjoy the ride. Alright Hilda, let it rip!"

Hilda pushed the petal to the floor, and the limousine accelerated rapidly to one-hundred and forty kilometers per hour. Gunther could see a large pothole on the road, and he felt the eight-passenger limousine with its armor plating and reinforced steel doors rise off the pavement as Hilda sailed over the pothole.

A powerful wind was chasing away the remainder of the clouds in the sky. Beech and Birch trees on both sides of the road, bent over from the force of the wind, seemed to be bowing down to the special soldiers of the Third Reich in a mockery of subjugation. They released their dead brown leaves whirling into the mercy of the wind as the limousine passed.

CHAPTER 2

November 15th 1944-Five miles west of Breslau, 4am

Ten minutes ago, Sally had landed in a farmer's field of tall damp grass, literally out of thin air. She didn't know where she was and hadn't planned to travel here; certainly not more than two-hundred and fifty years into the future. She stood up in the dark to see where she was and that's when the snarling Alsatian had charged over to attack. An elderly but tall and sturdy farmer was running after the dog to see what it had found.

Sally prepared to defend herself against the attacking dog. She had crouched down and aimed her laser derringer at the dog's belly as it flew through the air towards her. The dog let out a final yelp of protest before landing in an unconscious heap behind her.

"Halt! What have you done to my dog!" The farmer yelled into the darkness.

Sally listened and caught a few gruff words in what sounded like the German language. She could speak Russian thanks to the lessons from her mother, but not German. The farmer had become hysterical and was running towards her, so Sally fired her weapon and a bright white stream of energy briefly lit up the early morning darkness. The farmer crumpled up from the impact and fell, disappearing from sight in the tall grass of the field. Both farmer and dog would be unconscious for two hours, which would be enough time for Sally to leave the area before the farmer reported the incident.

Sally got up from her crouching position and brushed off her thigh-length brown robe and green pants. She gazed at the flickering lights of a town in the distance. It was damp, and the temperature felt like forty-degrees Fahrenheit, so she pulled the robe's belt tighter to keep the cold out.

Where was she. Sally looked behind her but all she could see, one hundred yards away, was an old wooden barn and a white stucco house fifty-yards behind it. It probably belonged to the farmer, including the field she was standing in. Sally had to take a breather after all that sudden action. She had to collect her thoughts and deal with her situation as she had so bravely done less than twelve hours ago in outer space. She would treat this situation with great caution. The buildings looked like those depicted on the tapestry at home, which meant she must be in Europe. This would be like another secret mission. Sally would not reveal where she had come from and act like she knew where she was going. She had to gather information without raising suspicion. Today's date and location would be the first thing she has to find out.

Sally looked ahead but all she could see in the darkness was a road about seventy-yards away. She started walking towards the road but after a couple of minutes she saw two bright beams of light to her left lighting up the road and the few trees that lined it on both sides. Sally stopped just ten yards from the road and hid in the tall grass for cover. A loud noise in the distance, a mechanical noise that sounded like metal gears meshing together, grew louder as the approaching beams of light bounced on the road and surrounding landscape. Sally saw fallen trees across the road in the next field that looked as though they had been hit by lightning. She wondered if one lightning storm would have struck down so many trees. Sally looked closer and saw enormous craters that had pock-marked the field, throwing up dirt and grass as though the land had experienced devastation from cannon shot.

Sally's concentration was broken by the noise of this mysterious machinery growing louder. The light beams had stopped bouncing on the road. To her left she saw the source of all the noise and a man standing on the road dressed in a strange dark uniform who had raised his hand for the machines to stop. The noise stopped and Sally could see the first machine was a black rectangular shape resting on four wheels with four men seated inside, two in the front, two in the back. They were dressed much the same as the man on the road. All five men were wearing a black hat with a small skull and cross bones above the visor. She wondered if they were pirates.

The men were speaking in the German language like the farmer. Behind them was a massive machine, resting on two large metal belts made up of individual steel treads connected together and wrapped around the drive wheels. All that moving metal on the road must have caused the noise Sally heard. On the top middle portion of this machine was what looked like a cannon. It was much larger and longer than a ship's cannon, and it began moving, swiveling in Sally's direction.

Sally ducked down in the tall grass, but she was too late. The man on the road had seen movement out of the corner of his left eye and immediately shone a light on her hiding spot only fifteen-yards away from his position.

"Stand up! Stand up at once, or I'll come over there and drag you out myself!" The officer on the road shouted.

Sally couldn't understand him. She slowly withdrew her weapon from the pocket of her robe, preparing for her defense.

The four men in the first machine watched with interest as the officer on the road called out to Sally.

"Hans! What is going on! One of the four men in the first machine yelled.

"I may have caught somebody hiding in the field! Maybe a spy! I'm walking over to investigate." Hans replied. He left the road and entered the wet field, training his flashlight on Sally's position.

Sally listened carefully as the sound of his footfalls crunching down the tall grass grew closer. The moon gave off enough light for Sally to check the minimum and maximum setting for the laser charge on her weapon. She stood up, quickly aimed her weapon at the advancing officer and shot him. He fell to the ground, his flashlight disappearing into the tall grass. Sally set the laser charge to maximum, firing at the larger machine with the metal treads and watched the laser charge surround it with a bright white light. The tank completely disappeared in a matter of seconds.

Sally yelled, "freeze!" in English, and pointed her weapon at the four men in the first machine. Two of the officers seated in the back had stood up with their strange-looking pistols drawn and pointed at her.

"Drop you weapons on the road, or you'll die like the big machine that was behind you!" Sally barked.

She moved towards them into the beams of the car so they could see her training her laser derringer on them. The commanding officer, Sally assumed, seated in the front beside the driver, could understand English. He told his men to drop their weapons. They obeyed his order, tossing their Lugers onto the road.

Sally looked behind the commanding officer and saw larger, taller vehicles with canvas covers running to the rear of the vehicle. She would later learn that these were called trucks. Trucks carrying troops, smaller staff cars and trucks towing large guns mounted on wheels. A convoy stretching for at least eighty-yards down the road. The two men in the first truck, were poking their heads out the windows looking with amazement at the empty space where the Panzer tank had been.

The commanding officer, Major Dietrich, spoke excellent English. He had been a spy for Germany, posing as a business agent for a well-established European company in New York while reporting back on American military capabilities.

Major Dietrich was thirty-eight years old, six-feet tall with an athletic build and had the blue eyes and blonde hair of the Aryan warrior that Germany, during this time period, had come to idolize. He looked down at Sally with disdain through those cold blue eyes that were deep-set in a face with sharp chiseled features. She was six-inches shorter than him, about seventy pounds lighter, with light brown hair parted in the middle and just long enough to cover the back of her neck where perspiration had caused it to stick. She was nervous about confronting her enemies and combat. Her hazel eyes were doing a poor job of hiding her anxiety. But, he thought, she was in possession of what must be a powerful secret weapon.

The major and his men continued holding up their hands while he introduced himself to Sally.

"I'm Major Dietrich and these are my men. We are only five-miles from our destination, which is a town called Breslau." He said emphatically, like an aristocrat.

Sally watched him carefully. He had a sharp pointed chin and a large hawkish looking nose which combined to make him look threatening, she thought.

"Why did you stop to attack me." Sally snarled angrily. She tried to sound intimidating.

While she waited for her answer, Sally moved the laser charge setting to mid-way, which would deliver six-hours of unconsciousness to the unfortunate offender. She didn't want to kill anyone. Sally wasn't aware that she had killed three soldiers in the Panzer tank.

"We thought you were a spy. Is that true. Are you here on behalf of a foreign government to attack Germany." The major asked in a calm voice.

"No, I was kidnapped and brought here, dumped unconscious in that field behind me." Sally lied.

"Why were you kidnapped. Who did this and where did it occur." The major asked in an incredulous tone. He somehow doubted Sally's explanation.

Sally knew she was in Germany. She thought about her response. It had to be convincing. She was becoming annoyed from the bright beams of their vehicle and shuffled to the left, closer to Major Dietrich. She noticed the eighty-yard line of vehicles behind them had turned off their lights.

"I know it seemed unlikely that someone would want to kidnap me, but I found it necessary to use my weapon for self-defense in Berlin. A drunk came after me and I shot him with my weapon. The kidnappers witnessed this and decided they wanted my weapon. Before I gave it to them, I warned them that the weapon would take off the unfamiliar hand of a stranger. Only the owner could safely handle the weapon. They didn't believe me. As soon as one of the kidnappers grabbed the weapon, his hand disintegrated, and he dropped the weapon and began screaming. Blood was pouring from the end of his right arm where his hand used to be. He ran off towards a building across the street to seek help. That left two attackers, and they tossed me in their vehicle and began interrogating me. They wanted to know if I could get them two more of these weapons that would be safe for them to use.

I couldn't speak German, but I shook my head, and moved my hands around and shrugged my shoulders. They finally gave up, knocked me over the head, and I woke up ten minutes ago on the field." Sally lied.

The major was almost satisfied with Sally's explanation. A weapon as powerful as hers might be the best protection in a desperate war like this, so he could understand the kidnappers' desire to steal it. In fact, the major was thinking about how he could steal it. Perhaps if he were to handle it with a pipe wrench. He would have to separate the weapon from Sally somehow, then hope a pipe wrench would not be recognized as a hand and disintegrate.

While Major Dietrich considered more of Sally's story, behind him, one-hundred yards away, Ivan Artemiev was creeping up closer. Ivan had run into the eighty-yard-long convoy on this winding road, about five-miles back. He had slowed down when he saw them, so that he was traveling one-hundred and fifty yards behind the last truck, with his lights off to avoid detection. He noticed the Panzer tank at the front of the column while driving around a bend in the road. He had become curious about this convoy. What could be their mission? As a spy he had escaped the clutches of the enemy and was returning to his superiors in Soviet-occupied Poland with valuable intel. Maybe he could add this to his list.

Ivan had seen the convoy abruptly stop at the top of the hill. Fortunately, he had come to a bend in the winding road and was able to park on the side of the road beside some trees which would help conceal the truck. Ivan got out of his truck and walked around the bend just in time to see the Panzer tank hit with a deadly laser beam. The laser charge covered the tank in bright light and in a matter of seconds it disappeared soundlessly into thin air, leaving nothing behind, not even dust.

Ivan froze in his tracks. Was the convoy under attack? If so, by who and was this a secret weapon? Ivan crept up cautiously. He was closer to the convoy, walking beside the ditch and shadows cast by a few trees to avoid discovery. Ivan was nearing the fourth truck down from the vacant spot left by the Panzer tank. He saw one of the soldiers sitting in the back of the troop carrier climb over the tailgate carefully and step on to the road. Ivan stopped to watch the soldier's next move.

Sally was waiting for the major to comment on her story. The major's men, the two dark-haired captains in the back, and the bald driver wore officer field caps like the major. They were cautious after witnessing the fate of the Panzer tank. And like the major, they still had their hands held high in the air.

"You can put your hands down now, but no sudden moves, or I'll shoot!" Sally snarled. She tried to sound vicious.

"Can you describe your kidnappers?" The major asked. He knew he was asking a question that would take Sally some time to answer. He was stalling for time trying to decide if this lady was British or American. The last choice he considered more dangerous.

"There were three men about six-feet tall with dark Mediterranean skin. The third man had blonde hair and was the one who ran off without a right hand and bleeding horribly. The remaining two men were dark-haired, spoke with strange accents, and were average build. They were wearing brown leather jackets and green pants with black shoes." Sally lied.

"The description of your kidnappers would match at least one-hundred suspects currently in Berlin. What kind of a car were they driving?" Major Dietrich asked.

The corners of the major's mouth had turned down and he was frowning. Something about Sally's expression made the major doubt her explanation.

An uncomfortable silence followed while Sally thought about an answer that might satisfy the major without revealing her lack of knowledge about vehicles in this day and age. Obviously, a car was the name for the vehicle the major was in now.

While Sally pondered, a couple of startled crows flew out of a nearby tree shattering the quietude momentarily. Unknown to Sally, a threat to her life was close by. The ambitious Rudolf Gruber had surprised the other eleven soldiers inside the canvas covered troop carrier when he got up and quietly made his exit from the truck. Corporal Gruber was a dark-haired, meticulously groomed twenty-five-year old who was hoping for a promotion. He had been an athlete before the war and, during combat training, had excelled in all the military exercises and war games. The over confident corporal poked his head around the back of the truck to see if the left side would offer more cover for his approach. He believed it would and set out creeping closer to Sally's position. His black steel helmet and long black coat helped to hide his presence. He was ready for the kill. Rudolf cradled a German MP-40 submachine gun in his arms, and carefully made his way down the side of the truck to get closer to Sally.

Sally had stalled long enough. She answered the major's question.

"I would say it was a vehicle like yours, except it had a top cover. I couldn't see any more details than that because of my struggle with the kidnappers." Sally answered confidently.

The major was instantly suspicious. She referred to the roof of the automobile as a 'top cover' and it was highly unlikely that the kidnappers would be in a large expensive car. But before he could comment, a sound broke his concentration.

Sally heard a sound like a boot crunching down on a small rock on the road. She moved swiftly to her right, where the sound had come from, and stared down at the darkened left side of the truck.

Rudolf looked down at the road and cursed his bad luck after stumbling on the small rock. When he looked back up again he saw Sally pointing her weapon at him. Rudolf fired his submachine gun, and Sally fired her laser derringer. Rudolf fell to the road unconscious. Unfortunately, Sally's left shoulder was hit by a stray round. It was only a flesh wound, but it caused Sally to flinch from the pain.

The major saw his opportunity, and he jumped out of the staff car to retrieve his Luger pistol. Sally caught this maneuver in time to fire at him, and he fell unconscious on to the damp road.

Ivan understood some English, and was surprised by the major's conversation with Sally. Who was this unusual enemy of the Nazis? He was also surprised that the bright beam of laser energy that struck both the corporal and the major, didn't cause them to disintegrate.

Could this lady control the intensity of the laser energy? Ivan had crept as close as ten-feet away from the empty space left by the Panzer tank. He got up from his squatting position and ran forward in an attempt to help this mysterious enemy of the Nazis. He was within two-feet of the major's unconscious body when he saw the other two officers jump out of the staff car to retrieve their pistols on the road. Ivan stretched his long muscular arms wide and ran at the officers, tackling both of them. They lost their footing and fell on the road, but one of them had managed to grab his Luger.

"Watch out!" Ivan shouted in his best English.

He had warned Sally while she was momentarily frozen, wondering what would happen next. She shot the officer who had his Luger trained on her and the other officer. She looked over at Ivan, grateful for his help and at the same time surprised by the sudden arrival of an ally.

Ivan held up his hand, pointing to the troop carrier. He didn't know how to tell Sally in English that there were other soldiers behind him. Sally understood and cautiously walked down the right side of the first troop carrier.

By this time, the soldiers had begun pouring out of the truck to help their commanders. Sally shot them one by one before they had a chance to train their guns on her in the darkness. Ivan reached into his pocket and pulled out his Tokarev pistol. He ran up to the next troop carrier and pulled back the tarp at the rear of the truck. He began shouting out in German for the men to come out of the truck and help their fellow soldiers. The men in the truck assumed Ivan was an officer and filed out quickly while Sally shot them from the opposite side closest to the ditch and Ivan emptied his 7.62mm caliber pistol from the left side of the truck.

Ivan was thinking that this mysterious lady had a weapon that was lightning quick and, judging by the way she handled herself, she had obviously been involved in combat before. She would be valuable to Ivan for the mission he would be presenting to his superiors.

One last troop carrier, thirty-yards away, remained and the soldiers had assembled on the road before realizing they had to run for cover. Sally was quick and lasered four of them and Ivan picked off two more who were running for the cover of trees on the opposite side of the road. Sally took one last look around at the unconscious soldiers then pocketed her laser derringer in her brown robe and turned to face Ivan.

"I speak both English and Russian." Sally said slowly, hoping he would understand. "Thank you for helping me." She added.

Ivan was buttoning up his brown leather jacket after putting his Tokarev back in the inside pocket. He looked at Sally with an expression of delight after her mention of speaking Russian.

"My name's Ivan Artemiev and I am lucky today!" You must be on a mission from the Kremlin. Is that Russia's latest secret weapon?" Ivan asked excitedly in Russian.

Sally was surprised and relieved that this person who had saved her from another gunshot could speak Russian. But what was he doing in Germany.

"Thank you, Ivan, for saving me from another wound. I'm Sally Zhiganov. To answer your question, I'm not on a mission. My mother taught me the Russian language and some history. But I'm not from the Kremlin. The Zhiganov's live in Siberia. Sometimes we go to visit them when we have a holiday. But it's been a few years since we last traveled to Russia." Sally explained. She had borrowed 'Zhiganov' from her mother's family. She remembered that last names were used in the 'outside world.'

"You have a rip on your coat. The left shoulder area." Ivan said with a note of concern in his voice.

"Yes, but this is just a graze. Maybe an angry red streak where a shallow furrow of skin has been removed. I suffered a worse injury last year when some damn pirate shot my left thigh. The doctor had to dig out the lead and it took an hour. Fortunately, the experience didn't leave a scar."

"A pirate shot you?" Ivan said. He was puzzled by Sally's story.

Sally realized her mistake and quickly made up a story from her mental list of half-truths. She must be getting tired.

"I fish with my father to help his business. People who like to steal the catch of the day we call pirates. They creep up alongside our boats and try to board. My father's family are fishermen, and sometimes they have to fight off pirates while fishing off the coast of Spain." Sally lied.

This explanation seemed to satisfy Ivan. "I see you have a special name for these criminals. I am on a secret mission for Russia, but while the mission was much more difficult than anticipated, I succeeded in getting valuable information for my country."

His broad and friendly Slavic smile was replaced with a frown. "I might have something for your wound which will prevent infection."

"Thank you, Ivan. That would be....Wait!" Sally stopped speaking.

She had noticed two soldiers running in the field, who must have been hiding behind the trees on the right side of the road. She ran over to that side of the road, bent down and took careful aim.

"They look to far away. Can you hit them from this distance?" He asked.

"The charge will spread out but still be effective up to five-hundred yards. If anything, it's easier to hit them. The drawback is they'll only be unconscious for half as long as the other men I shot. Only three hours." Sally explained while she concentrated on the shot.

Both soldiers were running in the direction of the small town in the distance. They were frantically running past blown up trees and around large holes in the field, sometimes falling in their rush to get away and report the attack.

Sally fired twice and, to Ivan's amazement, hit her targets from a distance of more than two-hundred yards, with a pistol. Both men went down, disappearing in the tall grass of the field.

Ivan was wide-eyed and impressed with what he had seen.

"That was great shooting! I think your weapon is very impressive; maybe a game changer in this miserable war."

"Ivan, this is a lifesaver, but it is also what I call a smart weapon. It knows its master and if the wrong hand is on the pistol grip, it will laser it off leaving the wound open and bleeding. One of my kidnappers found that out the hard way. As soon as I handed him my weapon, his hand was removed and his blood poured out on to the ground before he ran off in a panic. The weapon only works for me and is dangerous to anyone else wishing to steal it."

She was glad that Ivan had provided an open for her story, used again from her list of half-truths. This explanation would be an effective deterrent against theft.

"You were mentioning that the fleeing soldiers would only be unconscious for three hours, because of the weakening effect from the distance. So, the unconscious soldiers behind us will be unconscious for six hours. Is that correct."

"That is correct, Ivan. I would assume that the soldiers in the field would not return to this spot, but run on ahead to that town in the distance and report the incident. They will eventually return here with sufficient forces to investigate." Sally suggested. "How did you get here, Ivan?" She asked.

"I have a truck parked down the hill, under some trees on the shoulder, where the road curves down there." Ivan answered. He pointed in that direction.

"That's only about one-hundred yards from here." Sally said. She looked back at the head of the convoy and decided she had some unfinished business.

"I'm going to get rid of their staff cars and trucks. I don't want it to be easy for them to report us to their superiors. We need a head start to get away." She suggested.

They walked back towards the first larger staff car, the leading vehicle of the convoy. On her way, Sally lasered four trucks, causing them to vanish. There were two more trucks close to Ivan's truck that she would laser on their way back.

Ivan watched with fascination again as Sally stood in front of the large black staff car and fired. It briefly turned bright white before completely disappearing into thin air.

Ivan and Sally spent the next few minutes dragging the Nazis' unconscious bodies off the road and placing them in the ditch. Then they both walked down to the remaining two vehicles close to Ivan's truck. Sally stood in front of the first truck, its cab was empty and the driver's side door was open. She was about to fire at the truck but then held off, thinking it wise to check with Ivan before destroying the truck.

"Is there anything in their truck, like supplies we should have for our escape." She asked Ivan.

"Good thinking, Sally. Let me check the back of the truck. I think there may be a winter coat at the back of the truck which will help hide your brown robe. When the Germans report, they'll mention you wearing a brown robe." He explained.

Ivan walked to the back of the truck, pulled back the tarp, and there hanging on an inside hook was a winter coat that looked like it would fit Sally. Beside the winter coat was a full canteen of water. Ivan grabbed both items and returned to Sally. She tried the grey winter coat, and it was a perfect fit over her robe.

"Now you can get rid of the truck."

Sally fired, and the truck turned bright white for a few seconds, briefly lighting up the road and the few trees that lined it, before vanishing from sight.

Ivan felt that every time he witnessed Sally's weapon in action that he should pinch himself to be sure he was awake and not dreaming. Sally and her weapon were the best answer to what he believed could be a successful mission against the Nazis. He would approach this subject slowly so that Sally could carefully consider offering her assistance.

Sally and Ivan walked down to the last truck, which, on closer examination, turned out to be a flat-deck truck, carrying a rectangular-shaped container covered with a black tarp. Ivan walked to the rear of the truck and Sally followed behind with the laser derringer in her hand ready to fire. Attached to the black tarp was a yellow-colored notice written in German. Ivan read out loud his translation into Russian to Sally.

"This tarp must be left closed and secured, until General Zard is present to supervise its removal. This shipment's destination is New Berlin."

The notice didn't concern Ivan and his curiosity had got to him. He wanted to see what the Nazis were hiding. The container was close to fifty-feet long, but when Ivan removed the rear cover, he discovered it was a cage with thick bars running down to the other end where two large red eyes were glowing in the darkness watching

Ivan. He could see them blinking slowly, and he felt a quick chill run down his spine as he began to wonder what they had found. Sally had stepped over beside him and looked into the cage.

"Ivan, I think we need to stand back from the opening to be safe from..."

Sally didn't get to finish her sentence. Whatever it was that lay in the darkness came charging down to meet them. The cage and truck shook violently from each footfall. The black head of the creature was covered in raised scales that probably acted as natural armor to protect it. It had three horns that ran down the center of its head, and large jaws with four fangs arranged around the front of its mouth. The ears were frilled but not particularly large and the eyes were fiery red. Both Sally and Ivan moved back quickly from the cage.

"Ivan, that's what I would call a dragon. Right now, it's trying to decide who we are, which suggests intelligence. It hasn't opened its mouth and there are no signs of aggressive behavior yet."

The dragon continued observing Ivan and Sally. The moon provided enough light to shine on the cage, allowing Sally to see a row of sharp hornlets running down the back of its neck. The dragon's arms were muscular and large, and it was equipped with four six-inch claws on each of its enormous hands.

"Sally, how do you know so much about a creature that shouldn't exist?" Ivan asked.

Again, Sally realized she had slipped up. She came up with an explanation that might satisfy Ivan.

"Well, I would agree with you that it shouldn't exist, but when confronted with reality, I'm cautious. If it is intelligent, then it will look for a way out of its cage." Hopefully that would satisfy his question, she thought.

"I'd agree with that logic. Do you think your laser derringer will stop it?" Ivan asked.

Before Sally could answer, the dragon raised its neck and dragged it across the top of the cage, its hornlets that ran down its neck tore through the black tarp like it was butter. The tattered halves hung down in the cage, giving the dragon a view of the dark sky outside.

Overhead, the drone of a plane could be heard flying in the area, and the dragon seemed to be looking for it in the sky.

Ivan had already found the plane and identified it as a Russian Yakovlev, a Yak-7. It was a Russian fighter plane, and he wondered why it was so far into enemy airspace. A dangerous miscalculation, he thought.

"That's one of ours! A lone fighter plane that should never have strayed this far." Ivan said.

The dragon finally saw the plane and started to get excited. It dropped its neck so that its head was looking directly at the heavy chain and lock wrapped around the door of the cage. The dragon opened its hideous long mouth, revealing a black forked tongue and razor-sharp teeth. In the next instant, a blast of fire shot out past its ugly tongue and teeth and surrounded the lock and chain with fiery tendrils. The chain and lock fell to the ground after sixty-seconds of intense heat.

Ivan and Sally backed away to the other side of the road. Sally still had her hand in her robe pocket wrapped around the derringer. They watched anxiously, undecided about shooting or running, hoping the monster would simply disappear.

The dragon exited its cage, shaking the flat deck truck's suspension then with each footfall it shook the road. The dragon was a horror to behold in the moonlight. Its black raised scales gleamed in the light as well as the horn on the end of its tail, which was the size of an ice pick, and looked very lethal. It sat back on powerful looking haunches then without warning, sprung into the air flying at an incredible speed with its leather-like black wings.

Sally thought the dragon was at least thirty-five feet long, with two wings, each twenty-feet long. It tucked its large muscular legs up to its body and she saw huge four-digit six-inch clawed feet that must have been thirty-inches long. Sally could see that it was flying up to attack the plane.

"Ivan, I think it's going to attack the plane!"

The dragon had finally reached the fighter plane and one very confused and alarmed Soviet pilot. He couldn't believe what he was seeing. The dragon was flying beside him on his left only ten-yards from his plane. Igor Olshansky was glad he wore his parachute, because he had a bad feeling he was going to need it. He removed his flashlight from his utility belt and shone it on the dragon's raised black scales that covered the entire length of its body. At the end of its tail, a two-foot-long horn shone in the light. He estimated the dragon's wings were twenty-feet long giving it a wing span of forty-five-feet. They appeared glossy and leather-like, similar to those of a bat. The dragon's nine-foot-long neck was lined with sharp horn-lets and it swung over in Igor's direction. The hideous head and those large red eyes with their black vertical pupils seemed to be studying Igor. When the dragon opened its mouth, he saw four long fangs, shining from the beam of his flashlight and behind them sharp yet crooked teeth in a jaw the size of a crocodile.

Suddenly a deadly stream of fire shot out between those ugly teeth, directed at the plane's engine, causing it to catch fire. The propellers gradually came to a stop and the plane was beginning to lose altitude. The dragon flew around in front of Igor and he fired his cannon but it had been damaged by the fire. So, he fired his two 7.62mm machine guns but the one on his right-hand side only nicked the dragon. The dragon flew over Igor's falling plane and attached its huge black scaly arms around the rear of the plane's fuselage tearing off the rudder and horizontal stabilizers of the tail section with its feet. The dragon hovered in place stopping the plane from falling.

Igor slid back his cockpit's window and climbed out preparing to pull his chute's cord when he had fallen far enough away from the danger. He heard the squealing and crunching sounds of his fighter plane being destroyed and decided to bail out of the plane. He jumped out into the early morning darkness, just as the dragon brought its tail down with the horn on the end impaling the cockpit where the pilot had been a moment ago. The pilot looked up at the monstrosity, then deciding he had fallen far enough away from it, he pulled the cord for his parachute.

Ivan watched him land safely in a farmer's field. The pilot would have to be careful leaving enemy territory without being discovered. Ivan was also aware that the light from the burning wreckage might attract attention, resulting in more German troops being sent to investigate.

Sally had been observing the dragon which had finally broken the fighter plane into two parts. It tossed the remaining aft fuselage, which was burning, down to the ground and watched the front of the plane with its lifeless propellers fall behind it. When the dragon was satisfied with the destruction, it stopped hovering in place, and abandoned the area, flying in a southerly direction.

Ivan had left the concealment of the trees to witness a sight which seemed impossible. Sally, on the other hand, was familiar with what she had witnessed. Her enemy back in 1688 had been experimenting with these creations in order to use them as a combat asset in war. Now Sally was wondering about time travel. Her enemy was an immortal. This meant he could be using the Nazis in his quest for world domination. She looked at the crystal skull, which had changed to a gold bracelet attached to her wrist, as though it might answer her questions.

"Sally, I'm not sure what we have seen, but I'm going to forget this for now because it seems to have left the area." Ivan said in a shaky voice.

"We need to get back to my 'safe house' in Russian-held territory." Ivan continued. "No one will believe me if I report this. The pilot is probably thinking the same." He finished.

"I'm just as surprised as you, Ivan. We'll keep this experience quiet for now." Sally was prepared to act equally astonished.

Ivan and Sally walked over to the empty cage and flat-bed truck.

"The cage is only fifty-feet long, so the dragon must have curled its tail and neck then slept on its side leaving fifteen-feet of breathing room. The cage is twelve-feet tall, so it would have been cramped. But then it would probably be sleeping. All that gun fire probably woke it up." Sally suggested.

Ivan had no comment, so Sally lasered the truck and cage and they disappeared in a blaze of bright light.

"Lead the way to your truck, Ivan. I think we're finished now."

They walked the one-hundred yards down to Ivan's truck and Sally got in. She sat in the torn passenger seat and looked through a broken window into the back of the truck where a brown canvas covered the three coffins. There was just enough room in the back of the truck to accommodate four passengers on each side, albeit they had to rest their legs on the top of the coffins.

"Ivan, what's under the brown canvas?" Sally asked.

"I'm delivering three coffins to 'Lwow', Poland. We liberated this city from the German military in July of this year. However, I have become angry over the treatment of the Polish people by our army and secret police. I will quit Stalin's army, and secret police because of the atrocities they committed, after the war. But for now, the Nazis are a huge threat we must stop. I will trust you not to mention my feelings to my comrades when you meet them at our safe house in Lwow, where I can offer you shelter and food." Ivan explained.

"This is our cover story while we're behind enemy lines in case we get stopped. You will be my mute cousin come to help me make the delivery. I was supposed to use the coffins for three highly place Nazi women with special abilities that I had planned to kidnap and drug into an unconscious state, but the mission failed." Ivan thought a moment then said, "But right now, I will have to get the disinfectant for your shoulder."

Ivan walked around to the back of the truck and let down the tailgate and climbed in. He crouched low, making his way to a small supply box directly behind Sally. He withdrew a small bottle of brownish liquid that had disinfectant written in Russian on the label. He closed the small supply box and returned to the driver's side of his truck and got in beside Sally.

"I'll put this on your grazed shoulder wound. It will sting but will do until we can get to my safe house and have it dressed in a bandage."

Sally removed the left arm of the winter jacket, then the robe underneath so that her wound was exposed. Ivan took some cotton and poured the brownish solution on it, then dabbed it on Sally's wound. Sally flinched from the sting but remained still there after so Ivan could finish.

"That will hold for a while. We'll monitor it every three hours to be sure it doesn't infect." Ivan reassured her.

"Thank you, Ivan."

Ivan gave a quick nod of his head, then looked down at the key in the ignition of the truck and frowned. He held his breath in anticipation and turned the key. The truck's engine coughed and chugged its protest but eventually turned over, spitting out a large plume of dark grey exhaust fumes.

"Your vehicle does not sound good." Sally commented.

"I agree with you on that point. I am hoping it will get us to where we need to go."

Ivan engaged the transmission, and they rolled forward, driving up the hill and past the spot where the convoy's vehicles had been disintegrated. Sally looked over at Ivan. The beads of perspiration from his exertions had finally dried up, and he appeared to be relaxed. His short blonde hair was sticking up around his ears and his hawkish nose was running slightly.

"How do you plan to outsmart the German army, Ivan? I assume you'll select an alternate route back to your headquarters now that this incident has made you more visible." Ivan didn't answer, so she continued.

"I hope I haven't jeopardized your mission. The kidnapping caused me to miss my meeting in Berlin, and I'll have to make other arrangements in order to make a deal with a large customer for my father's fishing business." Sally lied.

Ivan turned to Sally with a surprised look on his face. He offered his broad Slavic smile, showing Sally two rows of gleaming teeth.

"That is very perceptive of you. And considering all the excitement you've been through, it is characteristic of an officer's instincts. You show a cool head with a logical question. But this is not the kind of behavior I would expect from a lady in the fishing business." Ivan said.

Sally was no stranger to covert operations as she had been involved in many recently, back in 1688. For now, Sally would have to hope that an opportunity would come up in their conversation which would tell her the precise date of the time period she had traveled to.

"We are going to travel away from the routes the Germans' would expect us to take for our escape." Ivan finally answered.

He reached into his pocket and pulling out a handkerchief, he blew his runny nose.

"Ivan, during turbulent times, I always assume a military posture. A military way of thinking. This is necessary for my survival. I mentioned we had to fight off pirates." Sally explained.

Ivan only turned towards her and smiled again, his way of showing he didn't believe her story.

Sally abandoned her explanations. She lapsed into silence and looked out her window at the ruined countryside they were driving through. She soon got bored with looking at the war-ravaged countryside, and she looked down again at the object that transported her into the future, now wrapped around her wrist. It had changed from a crystal skull shrinking in size to a gold bracelet when Sally arrived in the farmer's field. It had parked itself for safe keeping, on Sally's wrist after a leap into time. Promise me, Sally thought, that you will not allow a thief to steal you from me.

Sally looked up and, next to her, at Ivan as he drove. His talk of kidnapping was resonating with her. He had said something about three ladies with special abilities.

"Ivan, you mentioned three ladies you were supposed to kidnap. What special abilities do they have?" Sally asked.

"Hilda, Helga, and Ingrid are special elite soldiers of 'The Third Reich' and have participated in the 'Super Soldiers Project.' The project is responsible, through the medical injections they received, for giving them superpowers." Ivan answered.

"What kind of superpowers?" Sally asked.

"Hilda is a special test pilot for the Luftwaffe and, as a recreation for her, she is one of the top fighter pilots in Germany, boasting numerous kills since the war began. Helga is quietly referred to as a witch. Her psychic ability automatically turns on when there is danger. She locates the danger, the perpetrator, the weapons which are a threat, and tells Ingrid, who is able to shape-shift into a werewolf within sixty-seconds and attack the enemy. Helga is also what we call a mentalist, capable of remote viewing to see future events or, locating people, so it would seem from the congratulations I overheard." Ivan explained.

This was all familiar to Sally, especially when she considered the Dragon Queen back in 1688 and of course, here in this time, because she was immortal like the Wizard. But before Sally could comment, Ivan cut her off with his own question.

"Now tell me, where did you get such a powerful and advanced weapon as your laser derringer?" He asked.

"The area we fish in has a very colorful ancient history that goes back thousands of years. The well-studied academician can benefit from some of the treasure available and that includes ancient military technology now lost to the world." Sally answered.

"When you say ancient military technology, what are you referring to that is lost to the world?" He asked.

"The ancient craftspeople had specialized tools that could cut crystal without causing it to split or chip. For example; sound waves hold the molecular structure of a crystal together, so it won't split while the artisan is cutting it with the grain. If it is not cut with the grain, it won't function properly when used to store and release solar energy from the sun. The artisan knew where to cut the crystal into the proper shape so that it would store and release energy for the community and their home heating, cooling, industrial energy needs, and transportation needs."

"This technology is definitely lost to the world, considering the crude tools of the twentieth century. Where did you find it?" Ivan asked.

He noticed Sally's sudden expression of surprise at something he had said, obviously. But then she quickly changed back to the 'lack of luster' expression of a scholarly instructor who had taught the same lesson several times.

"My father and I are interested in archeology. We were in the Azores and that is where I found this weapon. We were drawn to the area by news of divers' finding a pyramid sitting at the bottom of the ocean close to Sao Miguel. Unfortunately, we didn't connect with our exploration team, which had the necessary diving equipment. We were on holiday and weren't going to let this mishap ruin our day. My father suggested we explore a remote area on the island. It was rumored that a strange old stone and marble building had become visible through many years of water erosion the banks of the shoreline had experienced." Sally began.

"After a two-hour hike, we found the building and began digging until we uncovered the entrance. We went inside and that is when I saw this weapon displayed in an ancient showcase beside a scroll. The showcase was very colorful, constructed with gold and an unusually bright orange-colored rock. The interior of the building reminded me of the interior of some of the Egyptian temples, including, hieroglyphics that were entirely unfamiliar to me. The stone walls were perfectly constructed and featured colorful ancient drawings of what I took to be the Royal family of that ancient time period.

There was no glass cover, so I simply reached in and grasped what looked like a gun, a pistol no larger than a pirate's derringer. I felt a strange sensation of energy flowing through my hands, down my arm, and all through my body. I began to panic and called my father over. By the time he reached me, the sensation had disappeared and I calmed down. I put the derringer in my robe pocket and we continued to explore the inside of the strange building.

After a couple of hours, it was getting dark outside, so we left the partially submerged building. The next day something came up to interrupt our holiday, and we had to leave right away. A week later we returned, but the building had fully submerged from a freak earth tremor and further exploration was impossible." Sally finished.

"That is an amazing story! I don't know how to comment on it, but I do know that the Nazis started an organization that looks for ancient weapons like yours. They hope that the discovery of such advanced weapons will help win the war." Ivan said.

Sally was already surprised by the mention of the twentieth century and even more astonished to hear that the Nazis were hunting for innovations like her weapon.

"How many more years will this war between Russia and Germany rage on, causing grief and suffering?" Sally asked.

"It has gone on for too long!" Ivan snapped. He caught himself and turned to Sally.

"I'm sorry, I must have lost myself. The war with the Nazis is a world war involving many other countries, and the misery will persist until we defeat these monsters." Ivan said.

"You know Ivan, that's alright, I understand. I think I need to close my eyes to rest. We seem to be the only vehicle using this road, but wake me if we're facing danger. Sally said.

"Good idea my friend. A little rest will help." Ivan replied.

The cab was silent except the chugging and rattle of Ivan's truck and the occasional pothole it ran over. Sally could feel herself drifting off to sleep.

"Sally. Saaalllyyy...Sally, open your eyes and look at where you are." A strange high-pitched voice told Sally to open her eyes and when she did, she was standing in midair on a sunny afternoon. Sally was floating, one-thousand yards above the old growth forest below and the 'Guardians' megalith castle in the distance. This was her home and she was one of four Guardians.

She turned to her right and there in midair with her was the crystal skull in its original size, gold in color. Sally looked at the lower jaw, noticing the crystal hinge. It was moving, speaking, and she listened to what it was saying.

"Your dream will only last thirty-seconds, but it will seem like thirty-minutes. I have brought you here and will help you now by showing you what is really happening in Azorka. Your friends and family have brilliantly out-maneuvered the Wizard's two-pronged attack against your home. Look across at your castle, and you will see your mother, the fierce warrior. She is chasing the Dragon Queen. Before you do, though, understand this, you are like a ghost and have no solid form, so you can not interfere with events unfolding around you. But, you can travel closer to see them."

Sally moved closer to the conflict. She somehow already understood that the Wizard had called for the kidnap of her sister. That was troubling and thought-provoking. How could they stand up to

Heather's telekinetic abilities, unless they hit her with a tranquilizing arrow of their own?

Sally's mom, Tamara, was on her Zapatsaur, a grey-colored fourteen-foot long flying reptilian.

Her long black hair flowed in the wind as she chased the Dragon Queen off the castle grounds. The Dragon Queen was flying directly towards Sally. She could see the expression of fear plastered on her beautiful yet horrid green face. The Dragon Queen was carrying a bow, so maybe Sally's hunch of an attempted kidnap was correct. The Dragon Queen flew right through her, unaware of her presence. Tamara was closing in and Sally could see her mom's fierce expression as she kneeled on the back of her Zapatsaur, holding a double-stringed bow with two copper arrows aimed at the Dragon Queen. She made her move just as Tamara fired her two arrows. The Dragon Queen's sudden shift downward in the direction of the mist blanketed ocean had saved her from the copper arrows. She would stay hidden inside the mist and return home to the Empire's island. Tamara decided to break off her attack, and returned to the castle.

In the next instant, Sally found herself standing in midair, above the Zapatsaur's mountain home. Beside her, twenty-feet to her right, hanging in midair, was her gold crystal skull.

"Thank you for helping me, my friend, for showing me what is going on at home." Sally expressed her gratitude.

The crystal skull didn't say your welcome but continued on with its presentation.

"This is the second attack. Your father and General Zen have fought off Gerta and her creature."

Sally looked just fifty-yards below her where her father and General Zen were kneeling on their Zapatsaurs and firing their lasers overhead at the strange-looking red-haired lady wearing a long green dress and riding on a flying creature. The creature was close to thirty-feet long, Sally estimated, covered entirely in black scales of varying size and with the leather-like wings of a bat, giving it a wing-span of thirty-four feet. The creature's head swung around on a long neck and looked at its attackers. Sally could see the unusual scaly skin on top of its head, which hung on top in several foot-long strands looking like some sort of freakish hair. The head held two lethal looking ten-inch tusks, Sally estimated, which hung horizontally, one on each side of its jaws. The sharp tusks hung past its mouth and could penetrate its enemy's skin up to seven-inches.

Up ahead, one-hundred yards to Sally's left, she saw an electrified circle appear in midair. In the next instant, the creature and the red-haired lady flew into its center and disappeared from sight. The electrified circle disappeared two seconds later. Mitch and General Zen broke off their attack. There would be no way to follow their enemy.

Sally wished she could call to her dad to let him know she was alright.

"Now you have seen what I can show you. I will be with you, Sally. I'm on your wrist and no one will be able to steal me from you. It's time for you to return and wake up. You'll feel refreshed. Ivan has a very important mission ahead. He'll ask you to join. It will serve the 'good in our universe' if you decide to help him."

Sally returned to the cab, feeling her body below her as she sunk back into it. She was leaning against the passenger side window and decided she'd sleep for an extra hour. She had witnessed what was happening in Azorka, and felt relieved by the Empire's defeat. However, her period of relaxation would be brief. Trouble would be waiting for her ten-minutes after waking.

CHAPTER 3

November 15th, 1944-Seven o'clock in the morning, six-thousand-feet above the ocean, five-hundred miles from Italy's south coast.

It turned out to be good early morning conditions for a secret flight out of Germany. Drifting clouds without rain or lightning.

Gunther looked out the small passenger window. He saw one of the two Messerschmitts on his side of the Folke-Wulf FW 200, acting as escort, should there be trouble in Italy's airspace.

The Folke-Wulf FW 200 was an all-metal plane with four engines that could reach a top speed of two-hundred and twenty-four miles per hour. The plane was armed with a 7.92mm machine gun for the nose turret, chin turret and the dorsal turret. The plane was well armed and this brought some comfort for Gunther. His heartbeat had returned to normal after the white-knuckle ride in the limousine with Hilda. She had been traveling over one-hundred miles per hour past the posted guards and their looks of amazement.

Passing over devastating potholes in the road. She had somehow caused the armor-plated, steel-reinforced limousine to levitate over them.

Hilda's severe expression and penetrating eyes bore into Gunther. Her unfriendly glance soon turned to a cynical smile as she could guess what recent experience Gunther was thinking about. She sat across from Gunther, her back to the two pilots in the cockpit, and took in his slovenly appearance. Helga was sitting beside Hilda, but she was concentrating hard on something with her eyes closed. She probably doesn't care about Gunther right now. Ingrid had laughed hysterically about his fright of high speed on their way to the Leipzig airfield. She sat beside Gunther and looked at him with her comical smile. "Gunther, what are you thinking about now?" She giggled.

Now that Gunther knew about Ingrid's shape-shifting ability, he was regarding her milk-white complexion as a feature she might share with the legendary vampire. However, Ingrid was the real thing and more frightening.

Gunther turned away from the window and looked at Ingrid sitting beside him.

"I'm thinking about the plates you found. They were crafted out of platinum which does not rust. But they must have been produced on Earth unless this platinum is from another world. Do we know if this material is Earth's platinum?" Gunther asked.

Helga opened her eyes and looked across at Gunther.

"That is an excellent question, Gunther, and I'm glad to see you're thinking about your contribution to the mission. The simple answer is

yes, we think the plates were crafted here on Earth because of the platinum material. When we have the translated message, thanks to your expertise, we'll learn more.

Helga looked around the comfortable passenger compartment that had been modified for this mission.

"Look, Gunther, at how considerate 'German Command' has been in regard to our comfort and security."

Thick and warm dark brown carpet covered the compartment and the matching leather seats were luxurious and comfortable. They had discarded their military boots and put on heavy wool socks tucked inside flat white one-piece snowsuits which they had zippered open, because of the warmth in the compartment. Underneath the snowsuit, they wore their white turtleneck sweaters.

"Four very special and fortunate soldiers on an extremely important mission and being flown by our best Luftwaffe pilots with two Messerschmitts escorting us until we have cleared dangerous airspace." Helga finished.

"When we're past the danger zone, Gunther, we should concentrate on getting some rest." Hilda suggested.

Ingrid and Helga were nodding their heads in agreement, and the passenger compartment returned to an uncomfortable silence for

Gunther. All that could be heard were the four engines of the Folke-Wulf FW 200.

While Gunther considered Helga's conversation and Hilda's suggestion of rest, up in the pilot's cockpit, Georg the pilot and Nickolaus, his co-pilot, sat comfortably in their high-back chocolate brown leather seats. They looked out on a cloudy day, the perfect cover for their flight. The Folke-Wulf FW 200 was performing well and Georg was glad he had the extra support of the two Messerschmitt's that were escorting them. When they were well past Italy's airspace, the Messerschmitt's would return to Germany. Georg would be left with the turret machine guns and one cannon. But he also had a new modification for Ingrid to operate. And this lady was a highly trained soldier with excellent records at the shooting range.

Georg had been present for the installation, and Ingrid's training on its operation. A small compartment with a door was constructed in the middle of the passenger's aisle behind him. Ingrid would open the door, then sit down on a seat behind two 7.92mm machine guns, welded and mounted together on a round piece of metal which could swivel three-hundred and sixty-degrees. She could manually move the two guns up and down to get her up and down angles. Then the plane's fuselage would open, and the compartment would rise and operate as a turret when the gunner was in place.

Georg looked over at Nickolaus who was gazing out his side window at the other Messerschmitt escorting them, flying beside them on the plane's right wing. For now, the Folke-Wulf looked like a passenger plane, but when the gunner's compartment was sitting above, and the covers removed automatically from the machine gun turrets and cannon, it would be a war-bird to be feared.

Nickolaus scratched through a healthy head of black hair combed straight back, to an annoying itch on top of his head. He looked over at Georg, who was brushing a lock of thin brown hair out of his eyes, while looking straight ahead at the cloudy morning.

"This is an important mission to our commanders. The four passengers are extremely vital to the success of the project in New Berlin. Nickolaus reminded Georg.

Fortunately, Georg was patient and understanding. He knew his co-pilot was fishing for more information, as if more knowledge about the mission would help him somehow.

"That is correct, Nickolaus. However, I've known you long enough to recognize your digging to see if I know more about the mission than you. The answer is no. I do not." Georg answered. He looked over at his co-pilot with a smirk.

"Yes Georg. I have heard some fascinating rumors coming out of New Berlin. Apparently, there are ancient ruins in New Berlin." Nickolaus began.

Georg was sure he'd get bored with the flight. No turbulence or air traffic. 'Luftwaffe Command' had done its homework. He looked out his side window and saw that the Messerschmitt pilot on his side was looking over at him, preparing to turn around. Georg had checked his instruments and could see that they were more than five-hundred miles past Italy. Both pilot and co-pilot respectfully saluted the two Messerschmitt pilots' as they left, returning to Leipzig. Georg brought the Folke-Wulf down a thousand-feet to fly under some cloud cover.

"Alright Nickolaus, let's hear some more about these Base 211 rumors." Georg said.

He had already heard that the previous residents of the buildings and the underground base area were 'ancient alien beings' who were estimated to be ten-feet tall. There was no shortage of rumors coming from this mysterious Base 211.

Nickolaus was glad he could get his pilot's mind off 'British Intelligence'. The British were in this area disputing land claims with a South American country. Their Lancaster's had been modified and could fly ninety-kilometers faster than the Folke-Wulf. They were armed with eight machine guns and often accompanied by a couple of 'Spitfires'. Of course, their Folke-Wulf had been disguised as a civilian passenger plane. Nickolaus continued with his story.

"Our expert engineers' and architects' adapted the buildings for living quarters to serve our commanders. The structural engineers' and architects' both agree that these ancient buildings were built to serve a taller and heavier advanced race of beings. The buildings are a work of genius in their design, technology and adaptability to the Antarctic climate. Energy was supplied by unusually large blocks of crystal found on the lower floor of each building. A special room was dedicated to the crystal which provided energy through a maze of lines to each individual room in the building."

"At the top of these wide five-story megalith buildings, a circular structure served as a sixth floor and observatory. The eight telescopes, one for each building, ran through the rock and iced roof twenty-yards above the building, then through many feet of rock to the surface. Our experts are still examining the apparatus and trying to locate the telescope on the surface. The eight buildings were constructed at the end of a tunnel in a large hollowed out area. Unfortunately, we don't know what kind of tool they used to cut this rock. They're arranged in a semicircle at the end of this tunnel, two-hundred yards from where we dock the submarine. This is the headquarters for our leadership, and located one-mile from New Berlin's east entrance used by our submarines." Nickolaus finished.

"That's an incredible story. I suppose this area is off-limits and that we'll not be invited on a tour." Georg said with a smirk. His sarcasm was too subtle for Nickolaus to register.

"Yeah, I think you're right about that, Georg. But I've been dreaming about forty-hours from now, when we'll be sitting down to some tender marinated sauerbraten beef, red cabbage, and sauerkraut..."

"Stop right there, or you'll trigger my own hunger, and I don't want to be drooling all over my instruments." Georg replied, bringing a chuckle from Nickolaus.

Nickolaus was gazing out the front windshield when he thought he saw a flash of light ahead of them. He picked up his binoculars without saying anything to Georg, and looked ahead. He was alarmed to discover a British Lancaster being accompanied by a couple of Spitfires on their flight path and flying directly at them, five-hundred yards ahead.

"Georg, we have British company ahead. We'll find out how effective our disguise is shortly." Nickolaus warned.

Georg was preparing to flick the switch that would uncover their turret machine guns and cannon the instant they were under attack. But for now, both the pilot and co-pilot remained calm.

Five-hundred yards ahead of Nickolaus and Georg, the commander of the Lancaster radioed the two Spitfires that were returning to base with him in New Zealand.

"Lion leader calling Arthur and Theodore. We have company four-hundred yards from here on our flight path. Wait for my order to attack once I've made a positive identification."

Trevor, the commander of the Lancaster, and its seven crew members radioed to both Spitfires. He never tired of the interesting assignments his ten years with the RAF had brought him. His forty-five years would have been well concealed in a face void of wrinkles, if he hadn't grown an enormous grey mustache which he kept waxed straight above a thin upper lip. He looked to his left where his co-pilot sat silently, exhausted from their reconnaissance mission.

"Take over Phillip. I have to use the binoculars to see if we have a challenge." Trevor said calmly.

He removed his goggles and put the binoculars to his eyes. This appeared to be a German Folke-Wulf passenger plane. Trevor knew all the tricks. He had studied all the latest enemy aircraft Germany could attack Britain with, and it would be a simple modification to weaponize a Folke-Wulf FW 200. Trevor wasn't taking any chances. It was German and Germany was the enemy. Civilians or not, it was coming down. Trevor put the binoculars down and reached for his radio.

"Lion leader calling Arthur and Theodore. Attack! Take down our German company."

Trevor knew that giving his Spitfire pilots the green light to attack was like releasing the hounds for a fox hunt. From the beginning of the war until now, those two had notched quite a number of kills on the side of their planes. The Spitfire had a one-hundred horsepower twelve-cylinder liquid cooled Rolls-Royce PV 12 engine that could reach up to three-hundred and fifty-miles per hour. They were both armed with eight wing mounted 7.7mm machine guns and would, Trevor thought, tear the Folke-Wulf FW 200 to pieces.

Three minutes before Trevor had given the command to attack, Ingrid and Hilda had been watching Helga closely. They knew by now, that when Helga closed her eyes, something was coming. On a mission like this, it could only be the enemy. Helga opened her eyes and looked directly at Ingrid. Ingrid knew that she would be the first called upon to get ready for an attack because of the turret, which would take time to enter and activate.

"Ingrid, get into the turret! We have a couple of Spitfires coming our way!" Helga said anxiously.

Before Hilda could get up and run to the rear turret to fire the machine guns concealed there, Helga called out for her to wait. "Hilda, stop! We're going to need you to stay close to the cockpit." Georg had seen the Spitfires break formation, so he hit the orange button on his dashboard. This would cause a light to flash a warning in the passenger compartment, and it would sound an alarm. Helga had beat Georg to it by three minutes, and Ingrid was already rising with the turret when the alarm sounded. Nickolaus pushed down the toggle switch that would release the machine gun turrets and 20mm cannon from their concealed compartments. Then Nickolaus looked up, for the last time, through the front windshield and saw the wings of the attacking Spitfire as Theodore fired a deadly burst of machine gun fire into the cockpit of the Folke-Wulf. Nickolaus and Georg were killed instantly.

Helga's psychic alarm bells were sounding off in her mind. "Hilda! We're needed in the pilot's cockpit!" She shouted out.

They both jumped up out of their seats and rushed to the cockpit, leaving a confused and shaking Gunther who was still buckling up in his seat.

Ingrid had gone through her transformation into a werewolf, then pushed the two machine guns forward through a slot in the glass of the turret. She gripped both handles for the machine guns with her enormous hands and claws. Ingrid was in time to see Theodore's Spitfire flying down and disappearing

from her view after its attack, which killed Georg and Nickolaus. However, Arthur was flying up from below to score a lethal shot at the underneath of the Folke-Wulf. He hoped to destroy the automatically operated machine gun turrets.

In the cockpit, Helga and Hilda have arrived to find Georg and Nickolaus bullet riddled bodies. Miraculously, the plane was still flying level and under control. Hilda unbuckled Georg and pulled his dead body out of the seat, while Helga unbuckled Nickolaus's corpse and dragged it on the floor behind their seats beside Georg. Hilda buckled up in the pilot's seat and Helga took the co-pilots seat. Arthur was flying closer to the Folke-Wulf's mid-lower gun turret, mounted beneath the fuselage, and took his shot which shattered the glass and destroyed the machine guns. Another blast from his opposite wing mounted machine guns, took out the cannon and chipped the glass on the rear turret, mounted beneath the tail of the fuselage, but currently without a gunner to operate the machine guns.

Arthur rose above the Folke-Wulf's tail, looked back at Ingrid's turret, and was shocked by what he was seeing. Ingrid's turret was occupied by what looked like a werewolf. A werewolf holding both handles of the two machine guns mounted in the turret, and firing at him as he passed. He was able to dodge the line of fire but not his curiosity. Arthur looked down and into the turret where he saw a white ski suit on the floor beside the rear legs and feet of a timber wolf.

He flew up to prepare for his dive with Theodore, and to pinch himself to be sure he was awake and not dreaming about what he had seen. Together they would shoot the Folke-Wulf down and take out the werewolf, which hopefully Theodore would witness.

Ingrid had gone through her change to be bullet-proof. She could do that and operate with the same decision-making skills that she possessed in human form. Unfortunately, if she smelled blood while in this state, the beast intelligence would take over. Under the circumstances, it was unlikely that blood would be spilled close to her while she was behind glass above the fuselage. Enemy bullets would be useless against her, and she could sit back all day long shooting at fighter planes. By now, Ingrid thought, Hilda would be flying the plane, and even if they shot both wings off, Hilda would keep the chunk of metal flying with her ability. But what bewitched Hilda,

Ingrid remembered, was being unable to move living things. Ingrid was wise enough to prepare herself for the inevitable 'dog fight' that Hilda would entertain herself with. Step one, for Hilda, was the projection of an invisible shield that would wrap around the cockpit protecting the pilot, co-pilot, and the windshield, from enemy fire.

Hilda was glad the Folke-Wulf's front windshield had held up with only four bullet holes letting in the wind. She would project her shield outside the craft, which would protect them and the glass. Sitting in the pilot's seat, she was beginning to feel the exhilaration of battle, and she could make the Folke-Wulf perform in flight those maneuvers it couldn't normally accomplish.

Hilda could see the flashing red lights on her dash that told her the machine guns and cannon were destroyed in Arthur's strike. Helga, as co-pilot, didn't need the instruments to tell her they had lost a 20mm cannon and the lower turret. Like Hilda, she wasn't concerned because they had Ingrid, who loved shooting.

The Lancaster was a superior fighter that was faster and more agile with eight machine guns and a crew of eight men. It came as close as fifty-yards away. Helga fired the automatic forward machine gun turrets, killing a gunner in the Lancaster's forward turret, just as Hilda banked sharply to avoid a head-on crash. She gained altitude in a maneuver the Folke-Wulf normally wouldn't be able to do. If Hilda hadn't been the pilot using her telekinetic ability, the Folke-Wulf would never have flown so fast with such dexterity.

Trevor was wondering what was going on. He thought his Spitfires had killed the pilots. What he glimpsed was a couple of glamorous blonde-haired ladies in those seats and flying like there was going to be a dog fight. His remaining forward gunner had kept firing as they flew by. He was upset, as Trevor, about the loss of a member of the crew. Trevor banked and turned the Lancaster around. He wasn't going to let the Spitfires do all the work.

"Men, we're going to take that buzzard down, no matter what. Give those machine guns a work-out and don't stop firing until you see billows of smoke pouring out of the Folke-Wulf." Trevor yelled.

Hilda watched the Lancaster make its turn and fly right back at her. So, did Theodore and Arthur.

"Theodore, I think we should wait until Trevor has made his pass, then dive on the Folke-Wulf. Over." Arthur suggested.

"Roger that. Arthur, I'm ready when you are. Just give the word. Over." Theodore replied.

The Lancaster was getting closer. Its 303 machine guns were blazing, all but one. Hilda was flying closer to the Lancaster and at five-hundred yards she suddenly dropped the nose of the Folke-Wulf, not to dive, but to give Ingrid a better shot. Ingrid took her opportunity and aimed her two machine guns. Her fur-covered massive hands never left the trigger. Sharp teeth inside her jaws showed as she growled from the excitement and nearly emptied both magazines, firing at Trevor and his co-pilot. She scored two hits and both Trevor and his co-pilot died instantly. She was delighted, let go of the machine guns, and sat her seven-foot hairy frame down, but not in time for one of Hilda's special aerial stunts.

Hilda suddenly pulled up in front of the Lancaster, narrowly missing a midair collision. She took the Folke-Wulf on a three-hundred and sixty-degree loop, allowing the Lancaster below to pass. Hilda heard a thump and a growl coming from Ingrid's turret.

Ingrid growled angrily.

"Sorry about that, Ingrid." Hilda called out her open side window.

Hilda banked sharply to turn, then fired the front turret automatic machine guns at the Lancaster's tail. She scored two hits on the starboard side wing-mounted engines which both began to pour out a black and grey trail of smoke, until it crashed in the ocean below.

Helga imagined by now that Gunther's mid-east-sun-baked complexion had turned very white. She smiled to herself, savoring his torment.

The Lancaster had gone into pandemonium briefly until one of the gunners had given up their post in the turret and tried to rescue the Lancaster by removing Trevor's lifeless body and flying the plane. But when Hilda had flown above it again, and fired the machine guns in the forward turret, it went out of control again. Dark trails of smoke poured out from two of the wing-mounted engines, but Hilda and Helga didn't witness the crash into the ocean. Another threat had captured their attention. Theodore's Spitfire was flying fast at them from above, at a forty-five-degree angle, eight-hundred yards away from the Folke-Wulf.

Theodore had been amazed to find two beautiful ladies flying the Folke-Wulf. But he was positively mystified when the Folke-Wulf accomplished the aerial acrobatics they were putting it through. Compared to the Lancaster, this was an overweight dog. Yet the pilot had it accelerating to gain altitude, at a swifter rate than what had been specified for the heavy passenger plane. Even more fascinating was the tight, three-hundred and sixty-degree loop it completed.

he Lancaster flew only ten-feet underneath it. After the Folke-Wulf had completed the loop, it banked sharply then fired its forward turrets, taking out two of the Lancaster's wing-mounted engines, which caused it to crash in the ocean below.

Arthur had radioed over and mentioned an unusual gunner in the turret mounted on top of the fuselage. He didn't know what to think. Arthur said the gunner looked like a werewolf or someone dressed in animal fur. Could Theodore confirm this?

Theodore was within two-hundred yards of his target, flying directly at Ingrid's turret, with all eight of his wing-mounted machine guns blazing. Some of the machine gun fire ricocheted off the fuselage, sailing past Ingrid's turret, but Theodore scored a hit on one of the Folke-Wulf's wings-mounted engines. The pilot side engine smoked and shut down. Hilda looked out at the damaged engine, smoke pouring out and the propellers no longer turning. She willed it back to health, using her telekinetic ability to repair the damage. The smoke cleared, and the propellers started turning again. There we go, Hilda thought, good as new. Now Theodore had seen everything. An engine that should be dead, seemingly repairing itself and turning back on sixty-seconds after being hit. But the most unsettling sight was the werewolf in the turret that Arthur asked him to corroborate for his report to the RAF. The head of this thing was covered in the blonde coarse hair of a beast, with hairy pointed ears. The elongated snout with fangs and burning red eyes that appeared to possess malevolent intelligence completed the nightmarish sight.

Both Arthur and Theodore would be spending some time with the doctors when they got back to RAF headquarters if they reported this.

The good news for Theodore was he wouldn't have to report this. The bad news was the black thirty-five-foot-long dragon, that seemed to appear out of nowhere. It gripped the fuselage from behind and started pulling the Spitfire upwards. The powerful Merlin engine was hit by a stream of fire pouring out between its huge jaws, causing the engine to ignite, smoke and stop. Smoke poured over the cockpit's glass. He checked the straps for his parachute, tightened the belt for the life jacket he wore then turned around. Through the glass he saw the hateful red eyes of the dragon staring at him and slender tendrils of black smoke exiting its flared nostrils. The monster was completely covered in raised black scales. The six-foot long muscular legs were straddling the fuselage while both of the twenty-foot long leathery black wings were moving rapidly. The dragon and doomed Spitfire hovered in the freezing morning air. The dragon's scaly black tail hung above the Spitfire with a long sharp horn waving back and forth. Powerful arms covered in raised black scales, rippled in muscle, and five-feet in length were gripping the fuselage only a foot away from the cockpit's glass.

Theodore kept his eyes on the dragon's tail and a good thing he did. The dragon's tail struck swiftly like a scorpion. He ducked lower in the cockpit, narrowly avoiding the lethal end of the horn as it tore off the cockpit's glass. Freezing air whistled around him, and he heard the machine gun fire of Arthur's Spitfire as he watched the bullets bounce off the dragon. Theodore looked down at the freezing ocean below.

Arthur had decided to break off his attack on the Folke-Wulf in an attempt to rescue Theodore from yet another incredible reality that would be hard to explain to RAF Command. Incredibly, machine gun fire would not kill the dragon.

Ingrid wasn't going to let Arthur get that close to the dragon. Arthur had continued flying towards the dragon, and began firing again. Ingrid fired and hit the Merlin engine so many times that the Spitfire began to smoke. Arthur stopped firing his machine guns. He couldn't see where he was going, the smoke was so thick. In a careless instant of confusion, Arthur was hit by Ingrid's machine gun fire. The Spitfire's propellers stopped, the plane dived, and with a trail of black smoke following behind, it crashed into the ocean below.

Theodore had seen Arthur's lifeless body, his head hanging to one side, going down to its icy grave. He turned away as the Spitfire crashed into the ocean. The dragon had withdrawn its tail, taking the damaged cockpit's glass with it. Theodore, after a quick prayer, jumped from his Spitfire, just in time to avoid a second strike from the dragon's tail.

Ingrid had watched the dragon destroying the Spitfire and had enjoyed the spectacle immensely. She started to shift back to human form and by the time the transformation was complete, the dragon had let the Spitfire fall into the ocean. She was standing inside the turret, naked with her white one-piece suit at her feet, and waving to the dragon that flew down to meet her.

The dragon flew beside the Folke-Wulf, only ten-yards away. Ingrid popped open the glass hatch above her, and standing on the machine guns, she poked her head outside, her long blonde hair blowing in the wind behind her.

"Dragon, I love you. Thank you for rescuing us. And thank Ignatius for us, and let him know we're on our way." Ingrid shouted above the wind.

Ingrid blew the dragon kisses. The dragon opened its jaws wide and released its ear-shattering screech, then flew away from the Folke-Wulf at an incredible speed, disappearing into the horizon.

Cruising at a comfortable two-hundred miles per hour, Hilda relaxed now that the threat was eliminated. She looked over at Helga, who had her eyes shut again.

"There goes Ingrid again. Calling Doctor Zard by his middle name." Helga opened her eyes. She had already figured out her dilemma and was ready to be social again.

"I know Hilda, but you know how she likes to tease the little doctor. Besides, when in public, she always salutes and respectfully refers to him as her superior officer, General Zard." Helga replied. "We all love the little doctor."

Ingrid had just opened the door for the turret, which had automatically returned to the middle of the aisle while the fuselage was being sealed with the sliding panel. She was fully dressed again and walked past Gunther, who was still buckled up, and looking a little pale.

"Gunther, you are looking too white. We are simply going to have to get more meat into your diet." Ingrid giggled.

"Didn't have time for introductions; that was a dragon. You'll meet the dragon again. I'll introduce you!" She smiled as she walked past him.

Ingrid opened the curtain to the cockpit and closed it behind her. "Poor, Georg and Nickolaus." Ingrid said with sympathy.

She reached up to the shelf and pulled down a large grey wool blanket. Ingrid covered Nickolaus, then Georg, shuffling them together under the navigator's seat to make room, then sat down. "That was fun!" Ingrid called Hilda and Helga.

"Yeah, I'll agree it was a fun morning!" Hilda turned around to face Ingrid.

"I know you enjoyed the aerial acrobatics and to top it off, 'dragon' saved the day!" Ingrid shouted over the Folke-Wulf's engines.

"Dragon is actually supposed to be sedated and on its way to Antarctica. Wonder what happened? I mean it's a good thing we had the help and that Doctor Zard had trained it to recognize enemy aircraft. But does Doctor Zard know it's free?" Hilda said.

"I doubt that he does, which means it somehow escaped or

was set free. Which in turn suggests the sedative was not strong enough. The dragon recognizes me and I sure did appreciate the help this morning. Ignatius said he'd make one for me when the fighting was over, but for now he needs to devote every available resource to winning the war." Ingrid replied.

"There's only so much we can do, but I'll radio New Berlin and let them know we were rescued by General Zard's dragon." Helga suggested.

Helga turned around and handed Ingrid a small package wrapped in wax paper. Ingrid opened it and her eyes flew open with surprise. "Major Wilhelm gave me that chunk of cold roast beef for you. I told him how you are always hungry after shifting back to human." "Thank you, Major Wilhelm." Ingrid shouted.

And that was all Ingrid said while she devoured the cold roast beef. During the dog fight with the Lancaster, Helga's ability had given her a glimpse inside Trevor's mind before he died. Trevor's mission was to drop two British SAS agents that parachuted out of the Lancaster and into New Berlin.

Helga would simply radio ahead to New Berlin and warn them of the possibility, as though she didn't know, suggesting that the Lancaster and two Spitfires could have been returning from a covert mission. And to expect one very hungry dragon to fly home to his master.

CHAPTER 4

November 15th 1944-ten am on a back-road heading towards Krakow.

The road was filled with pot-holes, so Ivan drove carefully. He wanted Sally to sleep peacefully. The sun had risen but so far it hadn't chased away a cloudy day. Maybe, Ivan thought, the absence of sunlight would help her sleep longer. He was certain of Sally's exhaustion and felt the sooner this was remedied the better. Her participation in a special military task he had been planning for the last couple of hours would give the mission a much higher probability of success. She was combat trained, in Ivan's opinion, and she had an advanced weapon that could recharge from the sun's UV rays. A couple of shots from the laser derringer could put those super ladies to sleep for easy transport back to Moscow. When they do find the large disc, the Nazis hope to have weaponized and flying, Sally could laser the craft, eliminating the threat. Maybe they could be back in Moscow in time for Christmas. For the next two hours, Ivan drove along the winding country road heading southeast. He drove past Gleiwitz, noticing the town folk walking through the rubble of past battles with the look of despair in their eyes. He passed a country orchard recently ravished by aerial bombing. The trees had some of their branches blown off by shrapnel, leaving the remaining branches reaching out in every direction in a time of misery, as though begging for mercy.

While driving through Sosnowiec, Ivan passed a German staff car leaving town. He gave a quick German salute to the driver, who was closer to Ivan than the officer sitting beside him. The officer turned around as they passed, looking at Ivan suspiciously then a brief expression of confusion appeared on his pale war-scarred face.

He must have concluded that Ivan was a local because he didn't order his driver to chase down his truck.

Ivan figured the officer wouldn't have been able to see Sally asleep on the passenger side. That may have tempted him to investigate. If that happened, Ivan would explain they were a day late for a delivery of three coffins for Krakow. We've been driving all night in order to get there as soon as possible.

They hadn't been reported, but in another hour, the soldiers would wake up in the field and make their way to the nearest town and report the incident. They have a description of Sally and Ivan. It will take some time to dispatch a German military team to hunt for spies. That team could include Messerschmitts and Stukas, and troop carriers with soldiers to search for them.

Ivan knew they would need to be in Krakow by then, and crossing a remote part of the Vistula River, to avoid capture. His plan was to arrive in Krakow, and find passage across the river with the help of a fellow agent. Once they were on the other side with the Red Army, they'd be home free and could carry on to Lwow and headquarters unchallenged.

The Red Army liberated Lwow from the Nazis on July 26th, and were sickened when they heard about the cruel treatment of the Jewish people in that town. In Kraków, a Jewish resistance group called 'ZYDOWSKA ORGANIZAEJA BOJOWE' was established in the Kraków ghetto in 1941. Ivan admired them for their bravery. In December 1942, the ZOB and communist partisans attacked and killed twelve German officers at the Cyganeria Café that was frequented by German Command.

Mentioning the cruelty of the German military to Sally, might convince her to help. Her participation in his mission will help liberate millions of innocent people suffering from this New World Order.

"Ivan, how long have I been sleeping for?" Sally asked. She looked out the front window.

Ivan slowed down and pulled over at the top of a hill, where the road offered a view of Kraków in the distance. Ivan looked to his left through a break in the trees which lined and sheltered the road.

"You've been sleeping for three hours. But that is good because we have arrived in Kraków. I need you to be awake for the German soldiers we must report to."

Ivan suddenly stopped talking. He thought he recognized a sound in the distance. Sally was about to say something, but he caught her. Holding his finger to his thin lips, he asked for her silence. Ivan listened carefully. In the distance, barely audible, he could hear aircraft. Ivan guessed a couple of Stukas were heading their way. That's what the dreaded sound was. The single engine of a German Stuka heading towards them.

From the field to his right. It was a deadly two-man dive-bomber that could dive at three-hundred and seventy-three miles per hour, and was armed with two wing-mounted 37mm cannons and a gunner in the cockpit behind the pilot. They could be carrying bombs, but Ivan thought it unlikely they'd waste them on this mission.

"Ivan, what's that noise I hear coming from that field to my right." Sally asked.

"That, my friend, is a German Stuka with a pilot and a gunner behind him, wing-mounted machine guns, and two 37mm cannons. They are probably looking for us." Ivan answered calmly.

"I can let it get close, then use my laser derringer. I'd need to climb those trees to get into a sniper position." Sally offered.

"That is very brave, but there isn't enough time to do that."

Ivan did a quick survey of the landscape. He looked at the trees Sally had mentioned.

"That field is open with a farmer's track leading to the copse of trees you pointed out. We can hide the truck under them and hope the Stukas miss us."

Ivan put the truck into gear and accelerated, moving the truck forward as fast as the old truck could manage. When they hit the field, using the farmer's track, Sally was jostled around on the seat as they made their way along the grassy path. He brought the charging truck to a stop between four pine trees.

The sound of the Stuka was getting louder. Ivan still had time to get out of the truck, race around to the tail gate and reach in to retrieve a ten-gauge shotgun from a hidden compartment in the truck. He had made some modifications to the double-gun's shells. The slug was much larger and there was more gunpowder used, which delivered a ferocious kick to the shoulder when fired.

"Sally, come over to the driver's side and crouch down behind the truck's tire. There's a chance the Stuka will not see us. And a chance the Stuka may sweep the copse with bullets in an attempt to flush out the enemy hiding there."

Sally moved over and took cover behind the driver's side front tire, crouching low enough for her head to be protected by the truck's front end. After three minutes, Ivan heard the two Stukas flying low over the field. He looked through the driver's side glass as they arrived flying over the hill. He saw their inverted gull wings a hundred yards away. The Stukas were not carrying bombs, but they had wing-mounted machine guns and a gunner behind the pilot in the cockpit. Ivan's second hunch came true, and the Stukas started firing their machine guns at the copse of trees where Ivan and Sally were hiding.

"Stay down Sally and keep your feet shielded by the truck's tire." Ivan whispered.

Machine gun fire ricocheted off boulders and then the truck. Sally looked down at the ground and could see machine gun fire skipping in the dirt around the front tire, then it was hit and started to deflate. Ivan was crouched down behind the driver's door and his feet were protected by a two-foot high boulder across from him in the grass on the passenger side.

Both Stukas had finished their attack and were about to turn around for a second run, so Ivan stood up and fired his ten-gauge shotgun at the second Stuka before it was out of range. He shot at the gunner in the rear of the cockpit before he could fire his machine gun. Ivan scored a kill and the gunner slumped down over his machine gun. He saw the surprised pilot turn his head, but cursed his luck as the second shot missed the Stuka's single engine. Not enough damage was done to eliminate the threat, Ivan thought.

"Sally! We have to move away from the truck and hide behind those two boulders, ten yards to your right!" Ivan shouted.

Ivan had made the right call in the nick of time. The two Stukas machine gun fire rained down on the truck. The front windshield was shot out. Three of the four tires were shot, and the radiator was riddled with bullets. Steam began pouring out around the engine's hood and front grill. Ivan's truck was rendered useless.

When the Stukas had finished their run, Ivan rushed out from his cover and targeted the pilot in the other Stuka before he got out of range. He scored a hit, killing the pilot, and causing the Stuka to go out of control. Before the gunner could turn around and rescue the situation, the plane crashed in the field, sending up flames and smoke into the morning sky. By this time, the angry pilot in the second Stuka was heading back for another run. Ivan had broken open his double gun to reload.

This was a matter of timing, Sally thought to herself. She decided to make her daring move. Before Ivan closed his loaded shotgun, Sally ran out into the open field with her laser derringer. The Stuka was swooping down, the scream of its engine getting louder, and it was almost ready to fire its machine guns. Sally ran towards the approaching Stuka as fast as she could, then slid under it on her back, and shot up at it with her laser derringer. The Stuka became a flying bright white image that disintegrated into dust ten-yards past Sally's position where she lay on the grassy field.

Ivan was amazed by her bravery and cool head. He looked over at Sally with a happy smile.

"Great shooting comrade! But come back over here, where we have the cover of these boulders and what's left of the truck. That was an SS officer you sent to Valhalla and there will be more coming over that hill in their grey jeeps." Ivan called out to Sally.

Sally took Ivan's advice, got up and ran back behind the cover of the truck's rear driver-side tire. She looked out from her position to the top of the field's hill, waiting for the enemy to arrive. Ivan remained behind the front of the truck on the same side, fully loaded. His two shots would hopefully count, and would be aimed at the drivers of the German staff car and jeeps. He thought for a moment then called over to Sally.

"Try not to hit the jeeps. We'll need to steal them for transportation."

Sally nodded her head in agreement, but remained quiet.

She was listening for the enemy and even thought it was possible for foot soldiers to come over the hill.

Ivan was crouching down, sheltered by the front of the truck on the driver's side, and its bullet-riddled flat tire. He had a good view of the hill from this position. Sally was huddled down on the driver's side at the rear of the truck, beside the back tire, the only tire that remained inflated. She was planning to laser a driver and officer when they appeared at the top of the hill. Then she hoped the vehicle would roll down the hill and eventually stop, providing them with transportation.

Ivan raised his head and a shot rang out, skipping across the front hood and narrowly missing him. He ducked back down for cover. Sally moved to the rear tailgate, looked around and saw a strange-looking small vehicle racing down the hill. An officer holding on to bars was saddled as though on a horse, with two wheels, back and front, under him. His machine was attached to a small cab, with two smaller wheels at the rear and one at the front. Inside the cab, an officer was firing at the truck.

Sally dove on to her stomach, avoiding the machine gun's bullets as they sailed over her. She fired her laser derringer at the contraption and in a couple of seconds, it became bright white and disintegrated along with both officers.

"That's a motorcycle and two more officers you have eliminated. Great shooting, Sally!" Ivan smiled.

"My pleasure, Ivan. But I was expecting a jeep, not this vehicle." Sally said.

Ivan's subconscious was tickled again. Mention of the twentieth century and the surprise briefly registered on Sally's face. Her combat readiness, and fearless behavior in combat. And now referring to a motorcycle as another vehicle. This all combined to create more questions regarding Sally's origins.

"You are very brave Sally. Your combat skills are extraordinary, and you have the instincts of an officer." Ivan said.

A nerve-wracking and silent minute went by before Ivan heard the sound of a jeep arriving. He looked up at the top of the hill where a jeep had stopped. It carried two SS officers in the front, and behind them in the back, another SS soldier was kneeling with a grenade in his hand. The officer in the passenger seat stood up and surveyed the area until his binoculars found the truck. He turned to the officer driving and pointed to Ivan's truck. He barked out a command in German and the jeep moved slowly down the hill.

"Sally, shoot the soldier in the back holding the grenade before he throws it at the truck." Ivan whispered anxiously. "Then change the setting to halfway and shoot. We're going to steal their uniforms." The jeep was accelerating down the hill and moving faster than Sally had expected. She saw the soldier in the back starting to stand up.

She moved out into the open and took her shot quickly before the soldier could throw the grenade, then ducked back behind the truck for cover. Behind the SS officers, the soldier turned bright white from the laser charge then

vanished from sight. The officer in the passenger seat, concerned about the possibility of a live grenade being dropped, had turned around in time to see him disintegrate with the grenade still in his hand.

"Franz, stop! There she is! We have orders to capture her!" The officer yelled.

The driver stopped, and the major jumped out and hurried over towards Sally's position. Ivan had to shoot the officer in the head in order to preserve the uniform. The officer's cap flew off undamaged, and he fell backwards on to the field. Before the driver could stand up and shoot over the windshield, Sally had moved her setting to half way and shot him. He collapsed unconscious in the driver's seat.

"Sally, grab the driver's uniform! It is small enough to fit you. I'll take the major's uniform. It looks big enough to be a fit for me. We probably only have five minutes before another motorcycle or staff car shows up at the top of the hill!" Ivan shouted.

Sally moved over to the jeep and dragged out the driver, allowing him to fall on the grass. She bent down and began removing the driver's uniform while Ivan moved out from his spot behind the truck, and removed the uniform from the body of the major. Sally had removed the driver's uniform in about three minutes. They were dressed in the coats, shirts, black pants, and boots of the SS officers. Sally wore the uniform of a captain, and had bundled her brown robe under the seat, putting the driver's uniform on top of her clothes. She looked as large as the unconscious captain lying in the field with just his white long-johns and white undershirt. Ivan had found the major's clothing a perfect fit. Unfortunately, there was a little blood on the white collar, but he had thought of a way to explain this. He handed Sally a white strip of cloth he had found.

"Here Sally, put this bandage over your ears. This will look like an injury from our struggle with the spies. Our story: I'm taking you to the other end of the city, where we will have the injury attended to by a doctor."

Sally took the white strip of cloth and wrapped it around her ears. Disguised now as someone who is deaf, she turned to Ivan for his approval.

"That's great. You'll appear to be temporarily deaf. The German guards will understand our urgency. The uniforms will help because of the reputation of the SS. You've seen how these animals salute, which you may be called upon to do. We're ready."

Sally moved around to the passenger's side and Ivan got in behind the wheel, slamming the door. Before engaging the ignition of the idling jeep, he had some orientation to cover.

"While we move forward on our way to Kraków, I'll need you to turn around in your seat and fire the officer's Luger as though we had an enemy firing behind us. The guards will witness this, making my explanations more convincing. Now pick up the driver's Luger and get used to the weight of the weapon."

Sally picked up the Luger and started swinging it around behind her to get used to the feel of the weapon.

"That is great. Now it will kick in your hands when you fire, so grip it tightly." Ivan cautioned.

"Our plan is to create a story compelling enough to make it to the river. A fisherman I know will give us passage to freedom once we've discarded our uniforms."

"Alright Ivan, I've committed this to memory." Sally replied calmly and gave Ivan the thumbs up signal.

Ivan engaged the transmission and with the tires slipping in the grass, the dark grey jeep shot forward. They rolled past the Stuka, still burning on the road with its pilot dead and face down on the pavement. Ivan stomped on the accelerator, and they crossed the road fast enough to be airborne briefly as the jeep touched down in the field on the other side, five-feet below the road.

Ivan reached down by his left boot and retrieved a grenade. It looked like a tomato masher. He tossed it behind him. The earth-shaking explosion was heard five-hundred yards away by the guards stationed to police the entrance to Kraków.

"Alright Sally. It's your turn to fire the Luger."

Sally turned around in her seat, and lifting the Luger up in two hands, she began to fire. There was some recoil, but it was manageable and she was comfortable with the feel of the gun.

"You're right, there is a kick, but I can manage it." Sally shouted.

Ivan accelerated even faster, making a show of driving recklessly, like he was running for his life.

After being jostled around from the ride in the field, he drove on to the rubble-strewn road which led to the guarded west entrance into the city. Sally took in their surroundings. They were on a road that had been bombed and shot up in past military campaigns and heading towards the guards, standing outside waiting for them. The gate was flanked by crumbling city buildings on both sides. It was eleven o'clock on a cloudy November morning, and she was still tired despite the fact that she already had a three-hour sleep.

"When we're only twenty-yards from the gate, I'll start speaking German, a sentence or two about your injury and I'll be calling you Hans. Remember you can't hear so don't respond."

"I understand, Ivan." Sally whispered.

She sat upright in her seat and frowned with a painful expression on her face. Her hair was well tucked up under the black SS cap and the white cloth wrapped around her ears, helped hide her hair. She arranged a few strands of light brown hair pulled across her forehead, just below the cap. It looked like this young man, an SS officer, had a military haircut as well as an injury that required immediate attention. The sun was permitted, by a thin bank of clouds overhead, to make a brief appearance. An unexpected flash of bright sunlight caused Sally to blink. When she looked up again, Ivan had begun speaking German out loud hoping the guards would hear him.

"Hans, we are almost here. Just hang on. We'll find some medical care on the other side of the city." Ivan shouted in German.

Sally looked straight ahead, frowning while facing two German soldiers holding submachine guns in front of the gate's barrier, which was fourteen-feet long and painted in red and white bands. This would be manually lifted from its position when the corporal approved the vehicle to enter.

The corporal had a set of binoculars dangling around his neck. He walked over to the two SS officers seated in, he thought, a dirty looking dark grey jeep which must have seen recent combat. The corporal would treat the two SS officers with great respect. He stopped beside Ivan, clicked his boots, and saluted.

Ivan returned his salute and introduced himself.

"I am Major Albert Ditters and beside me, Captain Hans Kempe. Hans has suffered a serious injury to both ears, and his hearing is severely impaired. I will rush him to another section in the city for medical care. We are coming from a battle with escaping spies, and we believe that most of them were killed in a raid on their position by our Stukas. You should be on the lookout for a Russian man and unusual woman traveling with him. She carries an advanced weapon, and we are trying to capture her alive. The Russian you can shoot on sight." Ivan explained.

"Yes sir. Please carry on through." The corporal saluted then turned to the private, standing beside the small booth on the right side of the gate. He gave the private the signal to raise the gate's barrier, which he did, then stood at attention while Ivan and Sally drove through.

Ivan drove past the corporal. He touched his black officer's cap with the death-head attached above the visor. A gesture of thanks to the corporal for his cooperation.

"Now that is what I call a lucky break. They didn't ask any questions. Just let us through. You are very convincing and obviously well-spoken in their language." Sally whispered in Russian when they were fifty-yards from the gate.

Ivan stayed focused on driving and the street. He accelerated, stared ahead, and whispered back in Russian.

"I think you're doing your part excellently, especially that hardened expression. For now, we are going to cut our drive short because I'm near to an area where my face will be familiar to soldiers who know me as a simple Polish farmer." Ivan spoke quietly; just loud enough for Sally to hear over the sound of the jeep's engine.

Sally said nothing in return. She stared ahead through the jeep's dirty front window and looked at the condition of the buildings ravaged by war. They were constructed of various colors of brick with stucco and some had a second-floor porch that looked out on a street with pot holes from bombs and grenades. Most of these buildings were bullet riddled and some had large chunks of construction blown away by bombing raids over the course of the war. Many of the windows had been damaged and some were boarded over. There were outdoor cafes, with fieldstone used for the walls on the lower floor and white stucco framed with dark wood on the second floor. They were easily identified by the outdoor arrangement of chairs and tables at the front of the establishment.

She closed her eyes for a brief moment and thought about her situation as it had unfolded. Sally had been handling a crystal skull. Without realizing it, she had activated its main function, which was time-travel. She was from an advanced civilization that had trade agreements with Atlantis recorded in its ancient history. The buildings she frequented included small pyramids, circular homes with a clear impact resistant domed roof, and a megalith castle she lived in. This civilization stayed hidden from the world, yet traded with the world in 1688. Sally's arrival here in the twentieth century was an accident.

She had recently discovered that the crystal skull was alive and acting in her best interests. This ancient piece of artificial intelligence was so much more, leading Sally to believe it was alive, with considerations for her own feelings and guidance while on this mission. She had been told by the crystal skull in her dream, that Ivan would be asking her to participate in a mission. The crystal skull had suggested agreement with Ivan, as it would benefit the 'good' of the universe.

Sally opened her eyes again. Looking at the depressed expressions of the Polish people they were driving past, she made up her mind. Sally would agree to help Ivan, in any way she could, in order to rid the world of the Nazi menace.

"We will have to find a convenient location to stop and change out of these uniforms." Ivan said.

Ivan turned off the main street and started driving down a side street. Up ahead he saw a dilapidated two-story red brick building with an old grey chimney that sat on top of a damaged roof.

Ivan turned into the building's small parking area and found a spot away from the view of passing traffic.

"This building is unlikely to be fully occupied, so I'm just going to change beside the jeep. You can have your privacy behind that septic tank at the end of this wall." Ivan suggested.

In less than five minutes, they had both changed into their original clothing. Sally wore the soldier's grey coat over her brown robe and green baggy pants. She welcomed her comfortable shoes. Ivan was ready with his old looking brown leather jacket and his worn black pants.

They left the jeep, making their way down an alley to a street Ivan had walked down before on his way to the river.

"I'm known as Stephan in this area. You can be my deaf-mute sister, 'Angie' as your identity, unless you can speak Polish."

They were walking down the street, looking relaxed. They blended in well with the few local residents, who shuffled along with them and across from them. The people payed no attention to Ivan and Sally.

"I can't speak Polish either, so that will be the best identity for me." Sally whispered back in Russian.

Sally took in their surroundings as they walked down a street that had somehow escaped the destruction of war. Outdoor balconies with planters for a variety of different flowers, strapped to the railings, gave the street color. City cafes had a large upper floor dining area for the restaurant and on the lower floor another eating area that extended from inside to an outside porch.

The windows were shuttered in different colors and not damaged. Brick and fieldstone were used for the lower walls, stucco with painted wood for the upper floor walls. Sometimes a red brick chimney could be seen. There were also brown and grey brick buildings built between the cafés on the street, that were untouched by the war.

A German soldier was walking up the sidewalk on the opposite side of the street. He stopped and looked over at them. He tipped back his metal helmet and when he called over to Ivan, Sally thought his friendly grin, was comical.

"Good morning Stephan." The soldier called across the street in the Polish language.

Ivan had known the young soldier for a couple of years, while he posed as a Polish farmer in Kraków.

"Good morning Max." Ivan replied in perfect Polish. "We're heading for the river and...oh...of course, this is my sister Angie. She is a deaf mute but has come along for the excursion at my urging. You know how tough war has been. She never gets out."

Max was clean shaven, with dark hair, probably about Sally's age, and stood six-feet tall in his uniform. He had a submachine gun strapped over his shoulder. When he smiled, Sally could see he had gleaming white 'horsey' teeth, with large gaps between each tooth. His happy smile, Sally thought, would provoke laughter.

But Max changed his expression to serious as he spoke to Ivan.

"Rumors are circulating about a planned strike by a resistance group.

So, I'm on patrol, looking for any signs of rebellion. The sight of you is like a breath of fresh air."

"If I see anything like a rebellion, I'll encourage the rebels to abandon their dangerous ambitions." Ivan assured Max. "Too many people, innocent people, could get hurt."

"That is absolutely correct. I wish everyone were as reasonable as you. I hope you both have an enjoyable day, Stephan." Max waved goodbye and carried on walking up the street.

After twenty-minutes of brisk walking, Sally and Ivan reached the river. Ivan hadn't planned to return to Lwow by coming through Kraków, but it presented an attractive alternate route. He had often helped an agent working this side of Kraków. Like Ivan, the contact spoke perfect Polish. His real name was Anton, and his cover name was 'Mieczyslaw' who made his living on the Vistula river, as a repair-man.

A square wooden sign, listing services in the small marine community, was attached to a street lamp by the entrance to the dock. It swung back and forth in the wind as Ivan and Sally passed underneath on their way to Anton's home. They walked by a few old wooden shacks in need of paint and probably some repair, that housed the few fishermen still left in the area, until they reached Anton's residence.

They walked down a couple of planks which led to the front door. It was in the same condition as his neighbors, and Sally thought it could use some paint and repair. Ivan knocked on a door so old and in need of paint, that it had become grey in color, and the wood appeared to be rotting.

The front of this wooden shack was painted a dark green and above the door was a sign in Polish. It read, 'Mieczyslaw's Boat Repair and Motor Rebuilding'. Anton was an expert at small boat repair and rebuilding motors for farm equipment in Russia. He had volunteered for this assignment, which was the monitoring of German shipments and troop movements in Kraków. Both talents gave him the legitimacy he needed to be living on the river and repairing farm equipment in the rural areas where German troop movements could be seen.

Sally watched as a man looked out from a dirty small window beside Ivan. The door opened and a stout man, dressed in grey, grease- smeared coveralls, stood in the doorway. Anton was five-foot seven, athletic, and weighed about two-hundred pounds. He had premature grey hair and a beard which helped conceal his youthful thirty-five years.

"Good to see you again Ivan!" Anton said in Polish.

Sally noticed a two-inch scar on his forehead, that crossed above his left eye. She assumed this was Anton's war scar.

"I'd like you to meet my friend, Sally." Ivan said as he turned to face Sally standing beside him.

Anton touched his heart with his right hand and bowed to Sally.

"I'm happy to meet you Sally. Won't you both please come in?" Anton backed up so that Sally and Ivan could walk into the two-room shack. Inside the room, dim light from a rear window high-lighted a small wooden chair in front of a table for four.

Anton and Ivan sat across from each other on crates, and Sally sat on the chair.

Ivan briefly explained in Polish how he had met Sally and what they had been through to get to the river. He told Anton that he was hoping for a ride down the river to 'Sandomierz' in the motor-boat. From there, another agent could help them get to Lwow. He emphasized the importance of the mission he would suggest to the Kremlin, and told Anton what he had overheard from the Nazis. He also mentioned that he would be asking Sally to join him but hadn't spoken to her about it because of her exhausted state.

Anton raised his hairy grey eyebrows in surprise after hearing this. He looked over at Sally and smiled as though apologizing for not including her in the conversation, then continued in Polish while Sally sat silently.

Sally understood the need for secrecy. If someone heard them speaking Russian, Anton's disguise would be compromised. This suited her just fine, as she couldn't add much to the conversation without the risk of exposing her lack of knowledge about the twen-tieth century.

Outside, the waves were gently splashing up against the poles supporting the rear of the shack. It was a hypnotic sound, and it helped put her to sleep in the chair.

"You know Ivan, the Koltov Corridor got chewed up by artil-lery fire and fierce German counter-attacks, but finally the 'Panzer Corps' were exhausted. We had them under constant artillery and aerial bombardment, and were able to circle 45,000 Germans, cap-turing 17,000 of them." Anton recalled.

"Yes, I have heard of our victory. I believe the German war machine is running out, and that the war may soon be over. The special projects the Nazis have are obviously what they depend upon to turn the tide. I'm counting on our leadership to give me approval for the mission. We'll destroy the super weapons they have in Base 211, to be sure we've put an end to the war."

"Apparently, I'm no longer needed for this outlook because of our recent victories. I'm returning to headquarters in Lwow, so maybe I can help by providing some ideas for your transport down to Antarctica." Anton offered.

"That is very kind of you. I would like to discuss all the elements of the mission which will be involved, and consider your ideas."

Anton rose from his crate. "In the meantime, I can make the three of us some coffee before we leave in another hour. I have a thirty-foot fishing boat outback tied to the dock. We'll use that to travel down the river to Sandomierz."

With this said, he got up and went into the only other room in the shack where he had a small stove to cook on and a small cooler to keep his food fresh.

Ivan looked at Sally peacefully sleeping and decided not to wake her. He gazed out on a cloudy early afternoon and considered some possibilities. Things had turned out well against the Stukas and SS officers on the motorcycle and in the jeep, thanks to Sally's secret weapon. However, Ivan believed that the SS would try even harder to capture Sally and kill him. They would send more fighter planes to hunt them down and would check the river if they discover the unconscious captain, and dead officer with their uniforms missing. The SS would check at Kraków's gate and the corporal would report that an SS major and wounded SS captain had passed through in the missing jeep.

Ivan's military theories were logical and left him feeling uneasy, like this was the calm before the storm. He felt around in his pocket and found the last two long-range custom slugs he had made for his ten-gauge shotgun. They would have to count and hopefully be enough to damage the engine of a Stuka, if they're attacked on the river. Right now, he had his shotgun broken down in two pieces and concealed on each side of his leather jacket in specially sewn pockets.

Anton returned with a tray containing three cups of coffee, some cream, and two large blocks of cheese for Ivan and Sally. He was certain they would need food. There was no sugar for the coffee, which was rare and expensive in Kraków.

Ivan reached over to tap Sally on the shoulder. "Hello Sally, we have something to eat and to drink before we leave, thanks to our host Anton." Ivan whispered in Russian.

Sally blinked, came fully awake, clearly embarrassed at having fallen asleep.

"I'm sorry I fell asleep. Is that large piece of cheese and drink for me? I can't thank you enough, Anton. I don't think I've had

anything to eat for the last twenty-hours." Sally said.

Her complexion was almost red with embarrassment from falling asleep.

"Well, you can work up a hunger killing Nazis. This is the best coffee and cheese in Kraków, for our Princess Sally." Ivan joked, whispering in Russian.

Sally smiled then reached for her coffee and the cream which she added until the drink was a light brown color. She took a sip of the warm drink and rolled her eyes with approval.

"That is a very tasty and warm drink, Anton. Thank you, comrade." Sally whispered.

Anton nodded his head and said, "You are very welcome. I was telling Ivan we would be leaving in another forty-minutes. I have radioed our contact in Sandomierz, and he will be waiting for us. I'll be driving the motorboat then coming with you. I'm expected at headquarters in Lwow."

"Anton is expected at headquarters because our leaders have canceled his post here. It is no longer necessary." Ivan whispered.

"You see Sally, during the Lvov-Sandomirez operation, Marshal Ivan Konev's 1st Ukrainian Front, liberated Lwow and captured a series of bridgeheads on the Vistula river. Since then, things have slowed down around here. Our enemies are no longer on aggressive footing. They've lost a great many military assets with no hope of producing more. Germany is concentrating on maintaining the front, but soon our overwhelming force will come crashing through." Anton whispered.

"I understand what you're saying Anton, and thank you for explaining this." Sally replied.

It was clear to Ivan that she didn't, but he wouldn't worry about that right now. Her polite manner was sufficient to impress Anton, who had come from an upper-class family in Moscow.

"I need to get rid of this boat and radio, so I've planned for the contact in Sandomirez to take it. Then we'll arrive at headquarters together." Anton said.

For the next five-minutes they enjoyed their coffee and cheese in silence. When they were finished, Anton took away their empty cups. He set down the tray on another empty crate parked just outside his second room, then called out to Ivan in Polish.

"I'm going out the back door to turn over the boat's motor, and get it warmed up for our departure. I'll be back in five-minutes."

"We are ready when you are Anton." Ivan replied.

As soon as Anton disappeared out the back door to the dock, Sally turned to Ivan, to let him know how sorry she was for falling asleep. "I'm really feeling bad about falling asleep, Ivan."

"Don't be ashamed of such things. As a matter of fact, I was glad you got some rest. I'm concerned about you, and I'm sure Anton doesn't mind either. I'm better rested, and used to going without sleep for long periods of time."

Sally looked at Ivan's eyes closely and could see the redness in his eyes. She stared at Ivan with a cock-eyed grin to playfully make fun of him.

"Comrade, if I didn't know better, I'd say you have a couple of cherries stuck in your eyes."

Ivan smiled politely at Sally's joke. They both sat in silence for the next few minutes until Anton came back from starting the boat's motor.

"I'm back and we're ready to go." Anton called out in Polish as the rear door behind him closed.

Sally and Ivan got up and walked over to the second room where Anton was standing beside the door. He opened it again and they left his shack, stepping out to a rear dock that served the small community.

Anton's thirty-foot fishing boat was running and tied to the dock. It looked clean and well maintained. The cabin was painted a dark brown, the same color as the boat's hull, and sheltered the controls, two upholstered seats and a bench behind them. Stepping over the rail, Sally walked around fishing nets and poles, scattered over a white deck smeared in mud and dirt from past fishing trips.

Anton walked past her, and took the driver's seat, and Ivan sat beside him. He had already untied the rope to the dock and was letting the boat drift until everyone was seated. Sally took her place behind them on the bench. Sitting behind the wheel, Anton moved the throttle forward and the inboard motor moved the boat away slowly. A thirty-foot fishing boat moving casually down the Vistula river, with as much urgency as a fishing excursion required. When they had traveled far enough away from the fishing community, Anton gave it more throttle. The roar of the boat's motor cut Sally off from conversation. She watched Anton and Ivan moving their heads side to side, up and down, in agreement or disagreement, as they shouted over the roaring motor.

Sally left the bench and wandered back out into the open, casually gazing up at a cloudy November sky. The motor's propellers were stirring up a wake in the ice-cold water of the river. Anton's craft was the only boat in sight that was carving a trail on a calm river.

They were traveling at twenty-miles per hour past homes, boathouses and over hanging trees close to the shoreline. The occasional fisherman could be seen removing his catch from his small boat, and sometimes children were playing close to the shore. The roar of Anton's engine caused everyone to look up and check what was making the noise, fearing another war machine, Sally thought. She noticed the relieved expressions of the children when they saw it was just a fishing boat.

But something was wrong. The tranquility she observed was too good to be true in times of war, and it left Sally feeling nervous.

They'd been very lucky to escape from the Nazis, yet Sally felt certain they would send a patrol of their flying craft, their fighter planes as they called them, to look for them. A casual glance upwards told her the sky was still empty, so she returned to the shelter of the cabin.

"Are you enjoying our trip down the Vistula, Sally." Ivan turned and shouted.

"Yes, very much, Ivan. It is very peaceful, so far. We've been fortunate, escaping the Nazis. I'm looking forward to rest, relaxation, and discussion when we reach our destination." Sally had to shout over the noise of the engine.

She had mentioned discussion, which she hoped would invite Ivan to make his request for help when they had stopped running. His stoical expression changed, and she saw his blonde eyebrows move slightly, above those deep-set blue eyes, at the mention of discussion.

Sally looked back out at the sky, and cursed her optimism. Maybe she had put a jinx on their day. Off in the distance, she could see two dark shapes that looked like fighter planes on patrol. She tapped Ivan on the shoulder, and pointed at the sky when she got his attention.

"I think we have company, Ivan." She shouted.

She withdrew her laser derringer, and placed the setting on maximum, while Ivan removed his ten-gauge shotgun from his brown leather jacket, assembling and loading his weapon with his last two custom shells.

Anton was looking for a way to deceive the Stukas. Fortunately, fifty-yards ahead, there were some over-hanging branches from trees close to the shoreline that he could pull under which might conceal them at this distance. He moved the thirty-foot fishing boat over and dropped his speed to a crawl so that the patrol would assume his craft belonged to a local about to dock.

Ivan turned around in his seat. "Sally, move in as close to us as you can. I don't want them spotting you. By now they have our descriptions." He spoke softly while the boat's engine was idling.

As Anton moved closer to the shoreline, Ivan looked up and could see the two gull-wings of the approaching Stukas. They were two-hundred feet above the river and the roar of their engines was getting louder.

Max was an ambitious Luftwaffe pilot. He brought his Stuka closer to the river, so he could get a closer look at the occupants of the thirty-foot boat which appeared to be docking. He wanted to be sure they were fishermen and not the spies they were sent to capture.

He was young, clean-shaven with dark hair, and was hoping for a promotion from Luftwaffe Command. Capturing this lady with the secret weapon, would definitely help his possibilities. But on this patrol, he was alone with no rear gunner to back him up. Germany was running short on military personnel.

Max peered through his binoculars at the fishing craft and if it wasn't for the unusual emerald green of Sally's pants, a description he had been given, he might have passed them up. He radioed up to the other Stuka pilot on patrol.

"Fredrick, I've made a positive ID on the lady's emerald green pants. Over."

Fredrick was a young blonde-haired pilot who didn't care about a promotion. He was flying one-hundred feet above Max and just wanted to survive the war, so he was cautious.

"Max, be careful with the lady. We don't know the range of her secret weapon. The Russian spies could be killed, but we have to capture her alive and seize the weapon. Over." Fredrick cautioned.

"Roger. I'm going to target the boat's engine compartment, which will probably result in the hull being punctured. They'll have to swim to shore to avoid hypothermia. Over and out." Max replied.

Max swooped down like a proud eagle about to seize its prey. The scream of the Stuka echoed across the river, shattering the serenity of the area.

Max felt the Stuka's engine accelerate, but he didn't want to dive too steeply. His target would be the boat's motor, and the Russian agent if he came out of the cabin with his shotgun. He looked through the glass over the cockpit and saw the light brown color of Sally's hair from one-hundred feet away, while she sat on the bench in the cabin. "Ivan. I'm going out into the open to take down the fighter plane." Sally announced.

Sally turned around and swung her legs over the bench. She got up quickly and rushed out into the open on the boat's deck.

Sally was positive that Ivan would object to her putting her life in jeopardy like that. However, there was a good chance the machine gun fire from the Stuka would hit the boat's hull, causing it to sink.

Before Ivan could object, which he did, Sally had moved out on to the deck and was pointing her derringer at the Stuka.

There she was, Max thought, and not bad looking either. He would make sure he didn't kill the lady with the secret weapon. The lady that destroyed two Stukas, a Panzer tank, two staff cars, four troop carriers, and a special delivery to Antarctica for Doctor Zard. But what Max didn't understand quickly enough, was the derringer the lady was holding up and pointing at his fighter plane.

The lady fired a bright beam of white energy at his plane, and before he could pull the trigger for his machine guns, Max felt a peculiar burning sensation, then a blast of bright white light filled his cockpit, and as he looked out on to the wings, his entire plane. Max had another thought left but no time to think about it. The Stuka disintegrated in midair, twenty-feet from Anton's fishing boat. "Fantastic shot, Sally!" Ivan yelled out from the cabin.

He had turned in his seat preparing to step into the open and fire his shotgun, but Sally had beat him to it. Ivan wondered where she got such courage. If she had been a couple of seconds too slow, the pilot would have pulled the trigger for the plane's machine guns and she'd probably be wounded or worse.

Anton had complete confidence in Ivan and Sally after the story Ivan had told him in Polish. He was astonished by what he had just seen. An entire Stuka and pilot disappeared in midair. Where did Sally get such a weapon?

Fredrick couldn't believe his eyes. Yet that is what the intelligence report's warning was about; disintegration. He was left briefly dumb-founded by the event and knowing he missed his opportunity to stop the boat, he pulled up into the sky in order to regain his senses and prepare for another run. He would roll his wings to distract her aim and fire at the boat's motor at the same time.

Ivan turned to Anton with a happy grin. "Welcome to our adventure, Anton." He joked.

Sally heard the whine of the other Stuka's engine as it got closer to the boat, and she took aim with her derringer. The pilot began rolling the plane back and forth, causing the wings to go up and down. He began firing his machine guns. He was one-hundred feet away when Sally fired and if it wasn't for her good marksmanship, she would have missed. Machine gun fire struck the water closer to the boat. The plane had been too far away for disintegration, but Sally's shot had torn through the starboard side wing, severing it entirely from the Stuka. The wing fell into the river twenty-feet behind Anton's boat. Fredrick couldn't stop the Stuka from going out of control with only one wing. Sally watched him crash into the river beside them.

The boat was moving along at a slow ten-miles per hour, fifty-feet from the shoreline. Anton no longer had the shelter of over-hanging trees but could see what looked like a copse of trees one-hundred yards ahead, so he decided to stay on this side of the river. He turned in his seat and stared at Sally, fascinated by her bravery and combat skills.

"Sally, why didn't you laser the second Stuka into dust, like you did with the first attacker?" Anton asked.

"Two reasons, my friend. First, I thought this pilot might start shooting from further away, having seen what happened to his fellow fighter pilot. Second, I wanted him to suffer! I am horrified by the suffering these Nazis have put the Polish people and other European people through, just because of their religion! I wanted this flying monster to freeze his ass off and hopefully suffer hypothermia from exposure to the ice-cold river!"

Both Ivan and Anton laughed out loud at Sally's choice of words.

"You made a good choice, Sally! They do deserve to suffer slowly. Maybe the pilot will have long enough to think about the suffering of war instead of the glory of war, falsely implanted in their minds by Nazi doctors." Anton said.

"Anton, there is one very special favor I ask of you." Sally said. "Ask away, Princess." Anton joked.

"I need you to keep your observations about my laser derringer secret until I've had a chance to explain it to the people we will be working with on future missions."

"That I can do for you, Sally." Anton answered.

Ivan was both delighted and relieved. He realized he wouldn't have to ask Sally to join him; she'd already volunteered. He detected a sense of patriotism because she had family in Siberia. But Sally's hatred for the Nazis was definitely motivating her to stay and fight with her compatriots.

"I thank you, Sally. I was hoping you would help us. How do you feel about Antarctica? Since seeing your weapon and combat skills, as I told Anton, I was going to ask for your help on a very important mission, when you were well rested."

"You mean the mission is in Antarctica." Sally asked.

"That is correct. However, I need to present the mission to our leadership for approval. I had overheard enough in the mansion that concerned me. I think our leaders will approve an attack on the Nazis' secret projects and super weapons." Ivan said.

"I'm ready when you are. Even if the mission's destination is Antarctica." Sally answered.

The sky remained empty for the next two hours. Anton had already moved to the other side of the river. He decided to travel at top speed, now that they were out in the open. The rumble of the boat's motor killed off the conversation between them while they day dreamed about hot food and rest.

They reached Sandomierz by four pm. Anton's contact was named 'Boris'. He was a six-foot, middle-aged, over-weight, and bald agent, posing as a Polish farmer.

Boris wore a dark brown canvas jacket with dirt stains on the jacket's elbows and it was missing a couple of buttons from his attempts to button it up over his pot-belly. He was a jolly fellow with a good sense of humor. He had looked at Anton's boat and assured him he could sell it, providing the new owner agreed to paint it another color. The Nazis would have its description.

The four of them were standing seventy-yards away from the river's shore, in an empty field. The small farm Boris used as a cover, was close by, and from there Anton, Sally, and Ivan would depart in another truck for Lwow. A rural farm house, five-miles north of the city served as a safe house and headquarters for special operations.

Sally glanced down the farm track they were standing close to and spotted a truck, leaving a trail of dust a couple of hundred yards away. Boris had also noticed their ride arriving.

"Your carriage awaits you, Princess." He joked with Sally.

Sally didn't mind a little attention and she liked Boris. She found him a jolly happy fellow as well as a compatriot.

"Is that beautiful vegetable truck my royal carriage which has been prepared to take me to my castle?" Sally teased.

"Indeed, it is!" Boris answered. When he smiled Sally could see he was missing a few teeth, which made him seem all the more comical. But, she thought, he was a good soul at any rate.

They climbed aboard in the back and Boris joined the driver in the cab. Ivan and Anton arranged themselves comfortably by shuffling bags of potatoes and other vegetables around. Sally had found a clear spot close to the cab's rear glass and sat down, prepared for another rough ride.

She looked over at Ivan and saw that he had fallen asleep leaning up against the inner wall of the truck. He snored between a bag of onions and a bag of potatoes. She didn't feel so bad about falling asleep at Anton's shack.

In another hour, they made the switch to a truck that would be taking them to the safe house, five-miles north of Lwow. Ivan will be reporting to headquarters in the city tomorrow morning after recuperating from this mission. The new truck had some bench seats in the back, and there were some blankets. Sally grabbed a couple of blankets to keep her warm for the next two hours. She enjoyed a comfortable ride.

When they arrived at the safe house, it was dark outside. Some light poured out from a living room window, and Sally could still see an old two-story farm house in need of paint and some repair. For now, it is utilitarian for the purposes of 'Special Intelligence'. There were some concrete slabs that were used as a walkway leading to the six porch steps up to the front door. The porch was only eight-feet long and six-feet deep, and the white paint on the wood was peeling and worn, just like the house's exterior where some of the wood siding was turning grey. The living room window looked out on the front yard's lawn, its brown grass growing in tall clumps, neglected and overgrown with weeds. The one tree in the front yard looked to be more than fifty-years old, and without its leaves, it looked lifeless and skeletal. Beside the tree, was a driveway and the truck Ivan would take to headquarters tomorrow, was parked there.

"Here we are, Sally. What do you think of our palace?" Anton asked. "It suits my needs. No complaints. I just feel like I need to sleep for a while. Thanks to your cheese, I don't need another meal." Sally answered.

"I will have a big breakfast ready for you in the morning." Ivan offered.

They walked up the steps to the front door and inside to a living room in need of plaster to cover the holes in the wall, and more paint. The floor creaked as Sally walked around the lower floor, becoming familiar with the layout of the house.

There was an old brown couch in the front room and four chairs, two upholstered in a threadbare, faded, old green material. The other two were wooden dining room chairs. The wood finish of the legs and arms were worn with scratches and spots where the finish had been worn off.

Ivan and Anton were seated on the couch discussing something as Sally walked past them to the staircase facing the front door. She climbed fifteen creaky steps and walked down a hallway to the first bedroom she saw and collapsed on the room's bed for a long sleep. And that's how November the 15th ended for Sally. A well-deserved sleep that lasted from six-thirty pm until seven in the morning the next day.

But some of Sally's dreams were filled with anxiety. In ten days, Sally will have completed her transition. She would have super abilities and have to learn how to use them. She might have some explaining to do because five days before that, her eyes would change from hazel to a dark navy blue.

CHAPTER 5

Six hours earlier. One o'clock in the afternoon, flying over the Atlantic Ocean.

Two hours had gone by since the fight with the British Lancaster and two Spitfires. Helga was relaxed in the copilot's seat but had her eyes closed and was concentrating on the two British agents that had parachuted down to New Berlin's ice-encrusted wasteland. It was that time of year when Antarctica gets more than twenty-hours of sunlight per day. Temperatures during the day were minus thirty-six degrees Celsius. Helga was hoping her psychic antenna would pick up the agent's thoughts, so she could zone in on them and their location. They were probably still too far away for this exercise to be successful.

Hilda had cruised two-thousand miles past Italy, and they still had six-thousand, three-hundred and fifty miles to go. They had to catch the British agents in New Berlin, and she was getting hungry for some hot food. Hilda knew she could push the Folke-Wulf faster. She would travel at seven-hundred miles per hour using her ability to increase the speed. The plane's construction had been improved and it was solid. However, if necessary, Hilda could hold together the plane's fuselage, tail and wing panels. The engines wouldn't be necessary. Now, New Berlin was only nine-hours away.

Ingrid was comfortably seated behind them and was preparing herself for a long flight. She would eventually decide to join Gunther in the passenger compartment. Hilda's seat was vacant, so she could sit across from him. She knew that Gunther had uncovered some mysterious ancient history and that would make an interesting conversation for the next couple of hours.

Gunther was still buckled up in his seat in the passenger compartment, wondering about the mission, and the ancient language he would be expected to translate. He was convinced, after what he had seen, that Hilda could pilot a large flying disc. If the disc is weaponized, it could win the war and this surely is what the leadership is expecting.

Back in the cockpit, Hilda had finally decided.

"Ladies and Gentleman, this is your Captain speaking." She began. "First the good news, we will be arriving in Antarctica by ten pm tonight, in time for a late dinner." She continued. "To accomplish this, we will be traveling close to the speed of sound. Gunther buckle-up, this will be one fun ride."

Gunther moaned, he should have known Hilda would pick up the pace but not that much. The wings and fuselage could lose some of their panels. The Folke-Wulf was not designed to withstand such speed, especially for nine more hours.

Ingrid had a suggestion. "Hilda, we should plug the holes in the windshield. I'll cut some material from the grey blanket here and hand up four perfectly round patches that your ability will hold in place while we're traveling that fast. It's bound to get cooler in here if we don't do that."

Hilda and Helga agreed with her and Ingrid went ahead and cut four round patches which she handed up to Helga. One by one, they were installed by Helga and held in place by Hilda's mysterious ability. The patches had become part of the plane's windshield and the air rushing inside was cut off.

"That is much better, Hilda. Good suggestion Ingrid." Helga said.

With that settled, Hilda began accelerating, but not before using her ability to shield the front windscreen from the pressure it would experience. The machine gun turrets were protected by sliding metal panels. They'd be ready if she needed them again. Then Hilda turned off her wing-mounted engines.

Gunther was looking out the window when he noticed the engine's propeller on his side had stopped. Shortly after that, the other engine's propeller nearest to him, had stopped. He craned his neck, and could see the same thing happening to the opposite wing. Hilda had purposely stopped them. Gunther's confidence in Hilda's abilities couldn't dispel his eerie feeling of the incredible speed they were traveling at. No longer was there a drone of the engines but the loud rush of air traveling at seven-hundred miles per hour.

"I'm going in the back to keep Gunther company, maybe take his mind off his fears by engaging him in conversation."

Ingrid got up from her seat and opened the curtain partition.

"Hello Gunther. Just thought I'd join you." Ingrid said as she walked in and took Hilda's seat across from him.

"By all means. Glad to have your company, and happy to hear we could have a late dinner in Antarctica. I don't think the crackers, cheese and cold meat will satisfy my hunger after so much excitement." Gunther answered.

"I guess you're not used to this much action in one day. I imagine after witnessing the unexpected, even the impossible, you'd be a little shocked." Ingrid said.

"I feel fine, Ingrid. I'm still getting used to the super-ability you ladies have acquired. It's a shock for an academic like myself to see fantasy abilities come to life when modern science can't explain the trans-humanism you three ladies have gone through. It's Doctor Wilfred Ignatius Zard's special project for the Third Reich, and it's a huge success with some incredible implications for the future."

"I agree with you, Gunther. We may win this war sooner, thanks to Doctor Zard. Only he can explain this type of biological hybridization. But then scientists need to catch up to his level before they'd be able to understand his explanations."

"I've had that experience in my field, when I encountered another archaeologist who was not well-read, and profoundly ignorant about the civilization being studied."

"What can you tell me about the Greek civilization? I've always been interested in that society." Ingrid asked excitedly.

For the next two hours, the conversation was interesting. Ingrid enjoyed hearing Gunther's observations and experiences. He had become more relaxed and Ingrid had burned off two boring hours of travel time.

At three pm in the cockpit, where the rush of air was loudest,

Helga and Hilda were both silent and concentrating on directing their abilities.

Hilda was focused on the Folke-Wulf's fuselage and wings. Using her ability, she was holding down panels, rivets, bolts, keeping the plane from falling apart from the stress of friction. Another part of her brain was entertaining her with thoughts about New Berlin and the large, mysteriously abandoned flying disc they had discovered in a valley. She could hardly wait to see it.

Helga was concentrating on the British agents, hoping she would pick up on their thoughts sooner. They could be a serious threat to secrecy and security if they are sending information by radio. The British are nearby with a post to keep watch on their land claims, but of course they would receive an agent's message.

Ingrid had slept briefly after a long conversation with Gunther. When five pm arrived, it was dark for a little while, then as they got closer to Antarctica the sky got lighter. By nine pm they were one hour away from Antarctica's sunset.

"Gunther, I'm wondering if you could help us when Helga locates the British agents?" Ingrid asked.

"Absolutely. What do you need me to do?"

"I need you to go up into the turret with some binoculars, I'll give you to spot the British agents. I'll let you know when. Right now, I'm going up front to see if Helga has picked up on them wandering around outside."

Ingrid got up and walked up front, pulling the curtain aside to join the other two ladies. Gunther was alone with his thoughts. He was feeling like a member of the team now that Ingrid had offered him this duty. He would do his best to find the agents.

Ingrid settled in her seat behind Hilda and watched Helga waiting for her to make a psychic connection with the British agents. The temperature in the cockpit had dropped a little. The sun was making its descent in the sky.

"We'll be arriving in forty-five minutes, Ingrid." Hilda called over her shoulder.

Ingrid nodded her head. She didn't like to compete with the noise in the cockpit. She thought the rush of wind over the fuselage at seven-hundred miles per hour was loud. Unfortunately, she would have to tell them Gunther was going into the turret.

"I have Gunther ready to be our man looking for the British agents from the turret. He'll use the binoculars while we're still flying towards them at a slower speed." Ingrid shouted.

"I still haven't located them but in another twenty-minutes, I should be able to pick them up if they're close to New Berlin." Helga turned around, speaking loudly.

"That would be a difficult hike for the British agents to make if they parachuted outside of New Berlin to avoid detection. They would already be tired walking from the area they parachuted into. They could be making their way through the Wohlthat mountains right now.

By the time we reach them, they'll be tired. New Berlin is a mountainous region." Ingrid spoke loudly.

Hilda called over her shoulder again. "The sun sets at ten-thirty pm and rises again by three am, at this time of year. It will be twilight by the time we arrive. If not for the British agents, we'd be landing soon. I would agree with Ingrid though, they are probably in the mountains somewhere."

Helga opened her eyes, turned to smile at Ingrid, then looked beside her to Hilda and asked her question.

"How much control do you have over the Folke-Wulf? Would you be able to hover in place then set it down on top of a mountain?" Helga asked.

Hilda was a little surprised by the question. This is exactly what she had been thinking for the last two hours. And she believed now that such a stunt was within the realms of her ability.

"Helga, if I didn't know better, I'd say you'd been reading my mind for the last couple of hours. But don't worry about that. We were orphaned together, grew up together and, as far as we are concerned, sisters. But to answer your question, yes, I believe I can. That would allow for a swift capture of the agents."

"Helga, it wouldn't bother me if you could read my thoughts, but this is a topic we can't discuss around our superiors. For some of them, this would obviously be a concern." Ingrid said.

"Our superiors would separate me from you two if they knew the complete scope of my abilities. They would isolate Helga if they even suspected she could read minds. We have to keep some things secret, guard our privacy." Hilda offered.

The ladies agreed to secrecy and the conversation lapsed into silence. Helga closed her eyes and went back to searching for the British agents.

The British agents were one-hundred yards from an eastern peak of the Wohlthat mountains and very tired from their eleven hours of travel. They decided to take a break and refresh with some of the water they carefully rationed out from their canteens.

Captain Nigel Harrison and Corporal Mike Farnworth were wearing all white ski jackets and pants over their green pants and black sweaters. They had trained for this mission so knew what to expect. The frigid temperature and sun set at ten-thirty pm were expected.

The captain was thinking it was an excellent time to pitch the small tent he carried in his knapsack. They could use the rest until three in the morning when the sun rose again. It was starting to get windy, and colder.

"Mike. I'm going to pitch the tent in this valley here for some rest and shelter from the wind. We can head for the top around three am." "That's fine by me. I could use the shut eye." The corporal answered. For the next twenty-minutes, they both worked at erecting the tent and securing it against the wind. When done, they crawled in and went to sleep.

Back in the Folke-Wulf, Helga broke the silence and yelled.

"I've located them. They're near a peak in the Wohlthat mountains, in a valley of the eastern range near the coast. They're putting up a tent for shelter and rest."

"Perfect, they'll be easy to apprehend for questioning." Ingrid said.

"I'm adjusting our direction and slowing down. We're almost there. Ingrid, this would be a good time to tell Gunther to get in the turret. By the time he's above, I will have dropped our speed to forty-miles per hour." Hilda said.

Ingrid got up and grabbing the binoculars, she opened the curtain and joined Gunther.

"Gunther we're ready for you to look for the agents. There's still enough light out there. The agents are resting in a white pup-tent in a valley that's near the peak they are climbing." Ingrid said.

Ingrid handed Gunther the binoculars as he got out of his seat. She watched him walk down the aisle and get into the turret. Before she could call after him to tell him how the turret worked, he had already figured it out, closing the small door and rising above for his surveillance duty.

Gunther felt the Folke-Wulf slowing down and when he felt it was slow enough to brave the wind, he opened the hatch. He stood securely on top of the machine gun's stand and poked his head outside after zippering up his hood and covering his face with a scarf. He focused the binoculars, which also helped protect his eyes from wind chill, and zoomed in on a distance of two-hundred yards. Nothing in sight just yet but he was in position and Ingrid was right, there was enough light for the task.

Ingrid wandered back up to the cockpit to see if Helga had found out anything more about the agents.

"Gunther's in place. He'll come racing down if he spots the agents and let us know where he saw their tent. Helga, do you have anything more about the agents, like what weapons they're armed with?" Ingrid asked.

"They are both sleeping right now. When they're awake maybe, but then we'll probably capture them while they're asleep." Helga answered.

The ladies looked down on the barren land of ice they were flying over. A nunatak poked out of the ice, large rocks were scattered about the landscape, and in the distance a glacier was visible. The Wohlthat mountain range was straight ahead, and coming up fast in the Folke-Wulf's windshield.

Gunther withdrew from the open air and closed the turret's hatch. He was freezing and realized he should have brought two scarves to protect himself from the temperature. He removed the scarf he had on, and cut four-inches off its end. He poked two holes, just large enough to fit over the binoculars. He got back into position and opening the glass to the turret he noticed a favorable difference. Hilda had slowed the Folke-Wulf down to an impossible forty-miles per hour as soon as they were flying over the peaks of the range. It had made surveillance for Gunther much easier to spot an off-white pup-tent the agents would be using, and report it on time. After a couple of minutes, he did just that. The tent was two-hundred and fifty-yards away. Gunther got down from his position and hit the down button for the turret. He opened the door to the passenger's aisle and ran up to the cockpit, opening the curtain. He was almost out of breath by the time he told the three ladies he'd found the tent.

"I found them. They're only about fifty-yards away now and probably directly in your path!"

Hilda brought the plane to a stop. She made the Folke-Wulf hover in place while she bent down and picked up the binoculars at her feet. Looking through the windshield in the direction Gunther suggested, she found them. One-hundred feet below, and about seventy-yards ahead, the off-white pup-tent was nestled in a small valley, one-hundred and fifty yards below a small peak. Hilda looked below through her side window. It was rocky, there might even be a hidden crevice they couldn't see. Then she spotted an area on the peak the agents planned to ascend, fifty-yards up from the tent. She could lower and rest the Folke-Wulf in place, while they capture them.

"I see a spot where I can set down fifty-yards above the tent." Hilda said.

She moved the plane forward slowly until the Folke-Wulf was directly over the snow-covered area between two large boulders which would prevent it from sliding down the incline. To manage this, Hilda lowered the passenger plane slowly, leaving the landing gear up and positioning the wings just a couple of feet ahead of the boulders. She set it down gently, the fuselage was cushioned by a thin layer of snow. The plane slid back two-feet until the wings rested on the boulders, then it stopped.

"I'll come with you, Ingrid, while Helga and Gunther make a couple of blindfolds for our prisoners." Hilda suggested.

Helga turned to Gunther, kneeling behind her close to the curtain. "Do you speak English, Gunther?" She asked.

"I'm afraid not, Helga." Gunther answered.

Ingrid had an idea. "I'd rip open their tent, right across the top and Hilda can yell 'surprise' and train her submachine gun on them. The sight of me and the submachine gun should be persuasion enough. We won't worry about the English language; Doctor Zard can take care of that."

Gunther went back to the passenger compartment to look for two strips of cloth they could use to make a couple of blindfolds and Helga followed him. Ingrid was already at the passenger exit door, and removing her snowsuit, preparing for her change.

Hilda walked in and when she saw what Ingrid was doing she stepped behind her to shield her nudity.

Ingrid screamed once, then growled as she shape-shifted into a werewolf. Gunther was tempted to turn around and look, but changed his mind. He felt the Folke-Wulf shudder from Ingrid's movements and was relieved when he heard the passenger's exit door open.

Ingrid jumped out on to the ice and snow-covered incline and slipped a couple of times as she made her way down to the tent. Hilda followed behind with a submachine gun cradled in her arms. They arrived at the tent. Hilda got into place with her submachine gun pointed down at the sleeping agents. Ingrid's right arm swiped across the top of the tent, her sharp claws tearing through the tent's material like it was butter. The British agents immediately woke up and froze at the sight of the werewolf looking down at them and Hilda's submachine gun pointing in their direction.

"Do you speak German?!" Hilda yelled.

"No, we don't speak German." Captain Harrison replied.

He nervously rubbed his dark brown mustache. Corporal Farnworth brushed a lock of light brown hair out of his eyes. Hilda reacted by training the barrel of her submachine gun on Mike's head. His eyes flew wide at the threat, and he remained still.

Hilda ordered the two agents to stand up by lifting the barrel of the gun upwards. They both stood up, fully clothed in their white ski jackets and pants. Ingrid towered a foot above them. She backed up, giving them room to step over the ruined tent. Hilda pointed with the submachine gun in the direction she wanted them to go, which was up the slippery incline, fifty-yards to the Folke-Wulf's passenger's door. Ingrid led the way and Hilda followed the agents, having to help them to their feet twice, after they'd slipped on the ice crust of the incline. They finally arrived at the passenger's door and Ingrid pounded on the door. Helga opened the door and Ingrid reached down and placed her enormous hands on Hilda's waist, lifting her into the plane while she trained her gun on the agents.

"Mike, I think that beast or trained creature, whatever it is, will pick us both up by the waist and place us inside that plane."

"Yes, captain, I believe we had better get ready for that." The corporal answered.

As soon as Mike had said that, he watched while Ingrid reached down and grabbed the captain by the waist, lifting him up for Helga to catch while Hilda trained the gun on him. He was next up and stood as motionless as possible while feeling Ingrid's hands and sharp claws wrap around his waist. The corporal was caught by Helga, who must have been extremely strong to be able to lift him the rest of the way onto the plane. They all backed away from the entrance, giving Ingrid room to board. She backed up, so she could take a short run, then hopped up and closed the door. Helga and Gunther placed the blindfolds over the agent's eyes and guided them to the seats in the passenger section, then buckled the agents in.

"I don't understand how they found us? New Swabia is six-hundred-thousand square miles." The captain said.

Helga yelled at the agents when she heard this.

"Silence! Silence!" She shouted her command in German, not caring if they could understand and prepared to slap them if they weren't quiet.

Both agents stopped talking, sensing the threat in Helga's tone. Ingrid had changed back while Hilda stood behind her shielding her nudity. She got back into her clothing, relieved by the warmth they provided. Tired from her transformation, she sat down facing the blindfolded agents, while Helga and Hilda returned to the cockpit.

After strapping themselves to the pilot's and copilot's seats, Helga turned to Hilda and expressed her concern.

"How do we explain the agents' capture? Do we tell them about your control over the Folke-Wulf?" Helga asked.

"I've been thinking that I have to mention everything in detail to Doctor Zard, our beloved second commander." Hilda answered.

"Good plan, Hilda. He will be pleased and surprised. More importantly, able to explain the unusual performance to the leadership." Helga said.

"I think Mitzi Zard is here with him, staying in the ancient buildings that have been converted for the leadership's comfort." Hilda said.

"I'm looking forward to seeing Mitzi." Helga said.

The Folke-Wulf slowly lifted off the incline and, after rising one-hundred feet into the ice-cold sky, Hilda turned on the Folke-Wulf's four wing-mounted engines. They started up with no problems and the propellers began to spin. Hilda moved the Folke-Wulf forward in the direction of the 'Schirmacher' runway. This was an ice-free surface for landing on the east entrance of New Berlin.

Helga picked up the radio set and announced their arrival to operators inside Base 211.

"We weren't expecting you so soon! I'll make the necessary preparations for our submarine to pick you up." The operator inside Base 211 informed them, over the static from his radio.

"That will be fine and thank you. By the way, we have captured a couple of British agents. Could you make some extra room on the sub?" Helga asked.

"Fantastic! I'll make sure you have an armed escort to deliver them. Over and out." A surprised operator replied through the radio static.

"I grabbed the agent's notes inside their knapsacks and put them in my pack before we climbed the incline to the plane. I'm sure there's valuable intel to be discovered by our officers who are able to read English." Hilda revealed.

"We might find out a little about their mission. I'm sure Doctor Zard, will get to the details using his hypnotism." Helga said.

"I'm looking forward to a great meal and some rest. As you know, we're staying in the ancient buildings. We have to walk through a tunnel for two-hundred yards to get there." Hilda reminded her. "That's alright, my legs could use the exercise after being in the Folke-Wulf all this time." Helga replied.

They were flying closer to the Schirmacher landing strip. After five-minutes Hilda began her descent, and safely set down on a narrow ice-free strip reserved for aircraft.

Hilda brought the Folke-Wulf to a stop. Helga left her copilot's seat to return to the passenger compartment. She'd slung her submachine gun over her shoulder by its strap. Closing the curtain, she joined Ingrid, Gunther and the two blindfolded prisoners. Helga looked out the passenger window and saw the German U-boat, U-530, waiting in the frigid waters for their arrival.

"We're here, and a short hundred-yards away to our right, is the U-530 waiting to take us down seven-hundred feet to the underwater entrance to Base 211."

The crew left the Folke-Wulf by the passenger exit, using the folding staircase this time, which made the prisoners easier to handle. They hiked over the rocky surface to the waiting submarine. Two armed guards sent to take custody of the British agents, were waiting on the short dock. Hilda discussed briefly with the blue-eyed, blonde-haired commander of the submarine, the unfortunate fate of Nikolaus and Georg. She told him that they had left their bodies behind on the plane.

The hatch closed on the submarine and, for the three ladies, the conclusion of a busy, fun-filled, November 15th at eleven pm. The last hour of the night saw them enjoying fine dining with the leadership, which included Doctor Wilfred Ignatius Zard and his attractive daughter, Mitzi Zard.

CHAPTER 6

November 20th 1944-'Special Intelligence' safe house, five miles north of Lwow.

"It's going to be another sunny day!" Ivan said.

He was looking out the cracked kitchen window, at a couple of surviving apple trees at the back of the yard with overgrown vegetation that covered their lower trunks. Ivan returned to the kitchen table.

Irina Volkov sat across from him at the kitchen table. The finish on the surface where they had both propped their elbows was worn-off and the chairs they sat on were rickety. The other four empty chairs rested on a black and white tiled floor that was, in some areas, worn right down to the planks. The walls of the small kitchen were covered in yellow wallpaper that had cracked and peeled over the old farm house's years.

"A perfect day to invite Sally to come with me to the library." Irina said.

Irina Volkov, was a twenty-seven-year-old 'Special Intelligence' agent. She had been working for the Kremlin based organization for the last three years. She wore her straight black hair combed forward and covering half her forehead. At the back it covered half her neck and she was often teased about looking like a Dutch boy. Irina had a healthy milk-white complexion, hazel colored eyes, and full red lips. She stood five-foot six-inches, with an athletic build and a black belt in Karate. Irina had also won several rifle-shooting competitions.

She worked in the communications room set up in a small closed in area across from the staircase, beside the front door. She was also the pilot for the mission they would all be leaving for in two days. Alfredo Mendez was the USA's contribution, and Haley

Ferguson was from Great Britain. Both Ivan and Sally would be leading the mission. Presently, Sally was worrying both Ivan and Irina. Certain physical changes in Sally, had left them feeling unsettled even perplexed.

"Have you seen how dark Sally's eyes are, Irina. Tell me what you think is wrong with her." Ivan said.

"The best way to find out is to ask Sally and see what kind of answer she gives us. She hasn't complained about any discomfort, and she doesn't want to see a doctor." Irina replied.

Sally was making her way down the staircase. She heard the tail-end of the conversation as clear as if they were standing beside her. Her hearing had improved incredibly over the last five days. She prepared herself for their questions.

"Good morning Sally!" A cheerful Ivan greeted her. His broad smile was welcoming. "I have a great breakfast for you, including two poached eggs, back bacon, and last but not least, pancakes covered in the most delicious maple syrup you could imagine."

Sally almost laughed out loud at Ivan's over-dramatic salesmanship. She took her place at the table beside Irina.

"Good morning Irina. What a beautiful day. We should get out on bicycles for some exercise after breakfast."

"I was thinking that too. A perfect day for another bike trip to the Library." Irina had met Sally two days ago, and they had gone to the Library together that day.

Ivan got up from the table, rolled up the green sleeves on his shirt, and started fixing Sally's breakfast. She saw that his light brown pants had a ketchup stain. Irina and Sally were both dressed in dark blue pants and white shirts. Sally would be careful not to stain her shirt. "How are your studies at the Library coming along, Sally?" Ivan asked.

"I'm reading about the 'Versailles Treaty' and curious about the reparation payments Germany is responsible for paying." Sally answered.

Ivan brought Sally her breakfast, steaming hot with the syrup in a separate dispenser. The poached eggs were done to perfection, not too hard, not too soft. And the back bacon was full of flavor. Sally dug in like a starving sailor, and for the moment, the room was silent, except for the echo in the kitchen created by her crunching her toast.

"Now that is what I call a great breakfast! It hit the spot and recharged my engines! Maybe you will have a hard time keeping up with me on the way to the library, Irina."

"It may be windy on the way. Would you like to cover your eyes with my sunglasses, Sally?" Irina asked.

"No, I think I'd be alright without them."

"You know, Sally, when Ivan first met you, your eyes were hazel, but now they are extremely dark, like the darkest navy blue. I remember thinking, when I first met you, two days ago, that you had unusually dark eyes."

"I have an allergy that causes my eyes to react this way. I've had this before, but it doesn't affect my eyesight. I see just as well."

"Would you mind if I tested your vision, Sally?" Ivan asked.

"No problem. How about after breakfast?" "That will do fine."

Ivan pulled out a piece of paper and began printing random letters in rows that gradually increased in size as he worked his way to the top of the page. The letters were in Russian, and Sally was glad her mom had taught her to read the language as well. Ivan got up and walked into the living room and tacked the test to the wall beside the kitchen entrance. He returned to the table and waited for Sally.

Irina looked over to Ivan when he was settled at the kitchen table.

"Alfredo and Haley are at headquarters loading the truck up with the last of the supplies for the mission. Did you hear that the Kremlin are giving us two customized sleds to travel on when we land?" She asked.

"I didn't hear anything about that, but it certainly is welcome news and will make our mission a lot easier." Ivan answered.

Sally was ready for the eye sight test.

"Before you two get tangled in a conversation, how about we do that test?" Sally said eagerly.

The three of them walked into the living room and stood twelve-feet away from the test, backing up towards the large living room window. Sally stood between Ivan and Irina. She knew they could not see the bottom row as the letters would be too small. But not for Sally's enhanced eyes.

"I will start on the bottom row and work my way up a row at a time. I'll write down my answers on a small piece of paper I was saving for my research at the library."

Sally withdrew her paper from a pocket in the blue pants she was wearing, and began writing down her answers. After a couple of minutes, she handed her results to Ivan. Ivan walked up to the test page and removed it from the wall and returned to the kitchen table to check it.

Irina and Sally looked like they were ready for a day at the office dressed in white shirts and blue pants. They left the living room and walked into the kitchen together.

They joined Ivan at the kitchen table, who was wiping spilled syrup off the sleeve of his green shirt, when they walked in. He was a little red in the face, but they wondered if it was because of the syrup or was it a sign of astonishment.

It turned out to be the latter.

"Sally got every last letter on the test correct." Ivan said. "That is something most agents, even our youngest pilots, could not have accomplished."

Sally thought he looked a little spooked, and Irina had adopted a similar expression. Nothing more was said, but much was thought about.

Sally left the kitchen and went back upstairs to get her grey jacket for the bike ride to the library. Irina said goodbye to Ivan, saying she expected to be back before nightfall. She got her red jacket out of the hallway closet and walked outside, waiting for Sally beside the two bicycles leaning against the outside wall.

"There you are, Sally. Could be a cool ride to the library with this wind."

"It will be a pleasure on a bright sunny day and great exercise." Sally replied.

Sally moved around Irina to get her bicycle, then they were both tearing down the driveway out to the road. Irina was ahead of her by twenty-yards on a road that hadn't been chewed up as much as the city streets. Sally soon caught up with Irina, which surprised her.

They arrived at the city entrance after fifty minutes of pedaling at top speed. The streets were chewed up in places but the rubble from the city's liberation in July was cleaned up. They pedaled past wrecked buildings being repaired and other buildings untouched by war, until they came to the library.

Sally and Irina walked up to the bicycle rack and parked their bikes. They walked up seven of the wide cement steps to reach the library porch and pulled the large brass handle for the front door. Inside the library, it was quiet enough to hear a pin drop on the dark brown tiled floor. The inside white-washed walls were well-preserved and the stacks of books were arranged in rows to Sally's right and Irina's left.

"I'm going to check our 'Geography' section to see what I can find about Antarctica's unusual climate, that might spark my curiosity." Irina said.

She disappeared down the nearest aisle and walked beside the stack of books towards the library's wide window. Sally turned to her right and walked down the rows until she found the 'History' section. She pulled out a small book about the 'Versailles Treaty' and walked over to a table and sat down to read it. This was Sally's favorite section, which had brought her up to date on the wars from Napoleon to World War One and now to the events that sparked World War Two.

After a couple of hours, Irina thought she should find Sally and see if she was almost ready to go. They didn't intend to stay longer than an hour and a half at the library today, but Irina became absorbed in her research on Antarctica, losing track of time. She found Sally sitting at one of the library's long wooden tables. Two more local residents, a man and woman in their fifties, were seated there, and pre-occupied with watching Sally read the books she had in front of her. She was turning the pages so fast, it made them wonder if she was remembering all the information she was reading.

Those were Irina's thoughts as well, and she decided to tactfully test Sally to find out what she remembered.

"I see you found the books on the Nazi party." Irina whispered. "This book would be helpful in explaining the phenomenon of their popularity. Have you read it already?" She asked.

Sally looked up at Irina and smiling, said, "That was an excellent source of information on those monsters."

Irina picked up the book and flipped through a few pages until she found what she wanted Sally to recall. She sat down beside Sally and turning to the eighth chapter, she asked her question.

"They really have some bizarre beliefs, like in chapter eight, which talks about the hollow earth theory. Do you remember that chapter, Sally?" Irina asked.

Sally turned to Irina with an over-confident smirk on her face and whispered what she had learned to Irina, word for word, as Irina followed the topic in the book.

"Well you certainly have a fantastic memory, Sally." Irina tried not to sound too amazed.

"We should get ready to go now if we want to be home before dark." Irina suggested.

"You're right, Irina, and I pretty much have got all the history lessons I need to learn about for the twentieth-century." Sally said.

Irina thought Sally's mention of the twentieth-century was unusual, as if she was learning the history for the first time. She got up and waited by the library exit while Sally returned the books to the shelf. Outside, they pulled their bikes free of the rack and made their way down the street towards the road leading out of the city. There were Russian soldiers patrolling the streets, and a large group of them had congregated a couple of blocks away. Sally and Irina were getting closer to the group. Seven soldiers were sharing a bottle of clear liquid. Sally was sure they were drinking Vodka. If they were drunk, they'd be trouble.

Suddenly, one of the soldiers, a young six-foot man who must have weighed two hundred pounds, all of it muscle, ran out onto the street

to confront Sally. He stepped in front of her on the road's shoulder, and stopped her by grabbing Sally's handle bars.

He let go of her handle bars and took off his helmet, tossed it over onto the sidewalk, and looked at Sally with blood shot eyes.

"Where are you going there my pretty girl? Why don't you have a drink with me?"

Sally got off her bike and let it fall onto the street. The soldier's lust showed in his smile. Sally was determined to wipe it off his face. She pulled back her right arm and hit the soldier in the face so fast that he was caught by surprise and fell to the ground. Mission accomplished; he wasn't smiling anymore. This brought howls of laughter from the other six soldiers who came rushing over to watch.

"That was a lucky punch, my sweet." The soldier managed to say while his mouth was bleeding from a couple of teeth Sally had knocked out.

Without warning, he raced towards Sally. She stepped to the side of the charging soldier, then came down hard with a chop to the back of his neck that knocked him out cold. Her martial arts lessons from Seiji and Ming back in Azorka had been beneficial, but she didn't expect the extra strength she had.

Irina had stopped and set her bicycle down on the sidewalk. She walked over and joined Sally. They were both the same height and weight, and trained in fighting.

"Ivan is right! You do have combat training! Excellent fighting, Sally!"

"I didn't think I hit him hard enough to lay him out unconscious though." Sally said with surprise.

The six soldiers were no longer laughing, and they moved in closer to Sally and Irina. She could see a serious conflict brewing.

"You are fighting against your own soldiers, we are with the Secret Service. Go back to your patrols, and I won't report this to your commanding officer."

This brought on more laughter and the soldier's drunken stuttering and slur of speech.

The soldiers had gradually edged forward some more during Irina's speech, and the one standing close to Irina, moved forward in an attempt to tackle her.

Irina rushed forward before the soldier could reach her, and jumping up she landed a painful kick to the soldier's left shoulder. The soldier fell back from the impact while Irina delivered a karate blow to the side of his neck, causing him to crumble unconscious in the street. Sally had two challengers lunge forward to grab her. With lightning speed, Sally took out the first soldier with a powerful punch to his stomach. The soldier gripped his stomach and fell to his knees gasping for air. She decided to humiliate the second soldier, and let him take several unsuccessful swings at her. She ducked from his last swing, then jumped up four-feet into the air and kicked him in the head. The soldier went down and stayed down. The first soldier was still winded from

Sally's punch to his stomach. Irina caught some of Sally's fighting while involved in her own struggle. The soldier she fought was six-foot two, and her blows to his head and neck were having no effect.

Sally turned around and saw the trouble Irina was having. She called out to the large soldier.

"Hey, you're a big ugly fool. Why don't you try me? I bet I can put you down in less than five-minutes." She yelled.

The soldier didn't like being called an ugly fool, it didn't sit well with him. The challenge was another issue, and an excuse to abandon his frustration with not being able to land a punch on Irina. The soldier turned around and faced his opponent. Suddenly, he took a swing, missed, and before he could take another shot at Sally, she had delivered a powerful kick to his stomach. He doubled over with the pain, just like the second soldier did, and Sally landed a blow to the back of his neck. He fell to the street unconscious. Irina had witnessed the fight, and wondered why her blows to the soldier's neck and head weren't that effective.

Sally and Irina focused their attention on the remaining two soldiers standing in the street. They were standing twenty-feet away. The soldiers drew their Tokarev pistols and aimed them at Sally and Irina. Sally's instincts took over and without knowing why, she raised both her arms and, aimed the tips of her fingers at their pistols. In the next second, Sally felt a peculiar sensation of energy running down her arms to her fingers.

Bolts of energy lashed out from Sally's two hands, each bolt like an electrical charge that hit the soldier's pistols at the same time, causing them to yelp from the electrocution, and drop their weapons.

Sally was amazed and realized her unexpected ability was all part of her gradual transition. She also knew that Irina was watching and probably shocked by what she saw. She turned to Irina, who looked at her with an expression of surprise at seeing the impossible.

"Let's get out of here before more soldiers arrive!" Sally urged. "I will explain everything when we get back to the safe house."

This was all Irina wanted to hear. She remained silent, still partially trapped in her own bewilderment, while they retrieved their bicycles and pedaled out of the city.

They arrived back at the safe house before dark. Irina had spent her energy on the fight and looked tired. Sally followed behind her. They parked the bikes against the wall and walked up to the porch where a smiling Alfredo greeted them at the door.

Alfredo was an American Marine. He was six-foot tall, with two-hundred pounds of muscle stuffed into grey sweatpants, and a black sweat shirt. Sally found him attractive but, of course, hid her infatuation. Alfredo was clean-shaven with black hair combed and parted neatly to his left side. His large brown eyes expressed his concern for the ladies when he saw them.

"What happened to you ladies? Your pants are scuffed and some buttons are missing from your jacket, Irina." Alfredo asked.

"I will let Sally explain the afternoon's events once Haley and Ivan have joined us in the living room." Irina said calmly.

Irina went upstairs to her room and changed out of her scuffed clothes. Alfredo walked into the kitchen where Ivan and Haley were sitting at the table discussing the mission.

Sally had a little dirt on her pants, so she decided to go upstairs and change. She reached for her freshly cleaned clothing from Azorka. The clothing in the twentieth century made her itch. And that reminded her, she would not reveal that she was a time traveler. Instead, she'll tell everyone that the crystal skull on her wrist was advanced technology that allowed her to teleport. They'd already seen a display of her laser derringer. It should be easy to introduce.

Five minutes later, Sally walked down the stairs, entered the living room and sat down on the torn upholstered chair facing the front window. Her comrades in the living room were seated and waiting for her explanation of the afternoon's events.

The room was silent. Sally looked over at Haley, dressed in a green top and brown pants and sitting on the old couch in front of the living room window. Haley had a fair complexion with naturally curly, thick brown hair that reached past her neck and was tied at the back. She was athletic, standing three-inches taller than Sally, and had extensive combat training. She also had a watch.

"Haley, what time is it." Sally asked.

"It is ten-minutes to eight." Haley answered. She had a beautiful voice that was slightly deeper than Sally's voice.

Irina was sitting beside Haley and had changed into beige pants with a green top. Ivan was sitting on the old dining room chair, and Alfredo was standing beside the fireplace. The brick work was crumbling.

Sally addressed the team in English for the benefit of Alfredo and Haley. Irina could speak English and Ivan was getting better at understanding English. "I promised Irina that I would give all of you an explanation for my behavior and the recent changes to my appearance."

"I'm sure you are all aware of the Nazi "Super Soldier Project" and that it has been successful for three ladies who are now in Antarctica. I have been exposed to a similar project. Irina saw me use one of my abilities today. After we roughed up some drunken soldiers, the remaining two men pulled their guns on us. I disarmed them with my new ability. I acted automatically, quickly, before they could pull the triggers on their pistols. I fired two electrical bolts at the pistols both soldiers were pointing at me, by raising my arms and using my fingertips to aim. The soldiers cried out in pain from the electrocution and dropped their pistols."

"The project I participated in is secret, but I can tell you from the beginning of the project to its completion, the maturity time varies for individuals. I have received my abilities in eight days. Now I have electro-kinesis, extra strength, agility in combat, enhanced hearing and sight, which Ivan has already confirmed. That's why my eyes went dark gradually."

"I'm glad you're on our side, Sally." Alfredo said.

"It gets better Alfredo. I'm actually going to return to my home and pick up four laser pistols which I'll train the team to use. We will need the extra firepower to disintegrate the Nazi disc Ivan heard about."

"It will seem like I haven't left this room. This gold bracelet on my wrist is the advanced technology that makes this possible. I will disappear right in front of you at precisely eight pm. In one more second I will reappear in front of you."

"Sally, it's two minutes to eight." Haley called out.

Sally nodded her head and continued with her explanation.

"I will shape-shift, looking like an amoeba, a single-celled aquatic protozoan, floating in midair in this living room."

"Thirty seconds, Sally." Haley called out.

Sally started the count-down. The room was silent. When she had counted up to ten seconds from eight o'clock, Sally called out loud, three special words. "Earth, ice, fire."

Sally heard a gasp from Irina and Haley as she shape-shifted in front of them. Ivan and Alfredo got up and stood three-feet away from her. All that the team could see, was Sally's face in the middle of a grey gaseous shape with a five-foot radius, holding a gold crystal skull in her hands. The grey shape was circular and rapidly rotating, changing shape by extending small projections of its gaseous consistency. Ivan saw that her gold skull bracelet was missing. Ivan could only see Sally's hands and wrists. Alfredo didn't know what to think, and, like the other team members, was mesmerized by what he was witnessing. After a minute had gone by, Sally vanished.

While Sally experienced the sensation of falling through a dark tunnel, she thought about her dream last night. The crystal skull had been speaking in her dream.

"Sally, we must return to 1688. The Wizard has subjected Gerta, Leif and Sam to his hypnotic process and equipment. We have to steal the equipment that breaks down barriers within the brain to produce super abilities and immortality. At eight o'clock tonight, I need you to initiate the trip by calling out loud three words, 'earth, ice, and fire'. The time in 1688 will be one o'clock in the afternoon. The Wizard's office will be clear, which is our first stop. Our next stop will be your home."

Sally felt the falling sensation slowing down. Suddenly, the darkness disappeared, and was replaced by bright afternoon sunlight. She felt her feet land gently on the luxurious hand-woven European carpet in the Wizard's office. It was empty, as promised, and Sally moved quickly over to the Wizard's desk and opened the drawer. She pulled out the helmet with the photonic crystal, then moved over to the screen sitting on the small table, and tucked that under her arm. She looked down at the crystal skull wrapped around her wrist and called out the three words again.

"Earth, ice, fire."

She converted back to her amoeba shape and in another

minute disappeared from the Wizard's office, arriving in the library of the Guardian's castle, her home. She pulled up a chair and sat down at the large table in the middle of the room. She placed the Wizard's equipment on top of the table and began writing her note to the other Guardians.

Mom and Dad, Heather and Lana;

I regret that I cannot come home just yet, and hope you will forgive me.

We have an ally. The crystal skull is more than alien artificial intelligence. It seems to be alive, and has been a watcher for thousands of years. It has decided to help us by working against the evil motivations of the Wizard.

I have received electro-kinesis, dark eyes like Heather, and by now, Lana. I also have super hearing, sight, strength, and can move quickly with super agility and accuracy in combat.

I am on my way to Antarctica to fight the Wizard. He is helping an evil dictator whose ambition is world domination. I am traveling with four special secret agents who represent the alliance against the dictator seeking to control the outside world.

I need to take the four laser pistols that Dad has stored in the library cabinet. I hope to return them when we complete the mission, but there is a chance I won't, depending on the outcome of the mission. I am traveling forward to 1944, where my team members are waiting for me to arrive at a farm house's living room. Don't worry about me. I'll be back for good when I complete the mission.

As you see, I have found it necessary to steal the Wizard's equipment. Heather, I trust you will explain the process to those who wish to become immortal, and perform the procedure. You have a choice to make Mom and Dad. To be immortal or remain as you are. Signed,

Sally, your Guardian 'Time Rider'.

Sally got up and went to Mitch's cabinet, taking out four of the latest laser derringers he had acquired from General Zen's research department in Azorka. She tucked two of them in each pocket of her emerald green pants and two more into each pocket of her brown robe.

With everything accomplished that she had set out to do, Sally called out those three special words.

"Earth, ice, fire."

Sally changed back into the amoeba shape in the library. Her large gaseous grey shape rotated rapidly, shooting out grey projections of its own substance. All that could be seen of Sally was her head and two hands holding the gold crystal skull, in its center. After a minute had gone by, Sally vanished.

She felt the sensation of falling through a dark tunnel as she traveled forward in time to 1944. In less than thirty seconds she touched down slowly, feet first, in the living room of the safe house.

Sally looked around the room at the shocked expressions coming from her four team members. Ivan and Alfredo were still standing three feet away from her.

Haley was the first to comment on what she had witnessed.

"That was incredible, Sally! It looked like you were floating down from the ceiling! It looked spooky."

Irina looked bewitched from watching the spectacle.

"Sally, that is absolutely amazing. Is this advanced technology?" Irina asked.

"Yes, it is. You will be seeing more advanced technology in Antarctica when we destroy the flying disc the Nazis have found. In 1936, a flying disc crashed outside a forest in Germany. The Nazis retrieved it and were able to learn more about the technology."

Alfredo asked his question. "Sally, do you come from an advanced civilization? I mean you went home by teleporting. You picked up four laser pistols, which I call advanced technology. Do you live in a secret society, hidden from the world?"

That is correct, Alfredo, and if we don't keep our society secret, the world will find us, overwhelm us and steal technology. This will endanger the planet and may even be responsible for destroying the Earth in a war.

Sally continued with her revelations. "What I have accepted is alien technology, a version of artificial intelligence. This is the gold bracelet which allows me to teleport, and has returned to my wrist. Our society goes back thousands of years. I'm sure everyone in this room believes that the building of the great pyramid in Giza was probably accomplished using advanced technology. Our civilization relied upon the pyramids that we built, to send energy through the Earth's magnetic ley lines before the flood."

"I guess you're not so spooky when you put all that into perspective." Haley said.

Sally emptied her pockets of the four laser derringers placing them on an old beat up coffee table in the middle of the room.

"Each of you will be handling advanced technology from my civilization. I believe these four laser derringers, will be more powerful than the laser derringer I have, so I'm just as excited to try them as you are in the morning."

Sally was satisfied with her discussions. So far, the team respected her privacy, and accepted her explanation of coming from an advanced civilization that remained shrouded in secrecy.

Irina spoke up. "I'm grateful for the advanced technology you have provided for this mission. I'm sure it will give us the advantage we need to stop the Nazis."

"Why don't we call it a night everyone and get some rest." Ivan suggested. "Tomorrow will be a big day for us!"

There was agreement, and a few yawns as they disappeared upstairs to their individual bedrooms. Ivan remained downstairs. He preferred sleeping on the couch, and knowing the lower floor was secure.

The last thing Sally thought about that night, while she stared out her small bedroom window at the moon competing with drifting black clouds, was Doctor Zard. She remembered the day Ivan had told her new information about Wilfred Ignatius Zard. Of course, by then Sally had already figured out his identity. It made sense that the immortal Wizard would also be in the future. Ivan had told her that Doctor Zard and his psychic daughter, Mitzi Zard, are the masterminds behind psychic sessions for the leadership of the Nazis. Sally knew what was going on. She recognized that it was a deliberate fake and illusion, in order to sway the leadership in the direction the Wizard wanted to take them in. He...would...be... And that was the last thing Sally thought, before she drifted off to sleep.

In her dream, a friend she recognized was speaking to her softly, reassuring her of the mission's success.

"Rest now, my young heroine. The mission will be successful. But I want you to see the evil of the Wizard. Without his help, the Nazis would never have been able to build Base 211."

"The daring confiscation of the Wizard's equipment tonight was a success. I remained on your wrist while we teleported to the Guardian's castle. Then while we were there, you unloaded the Wizard's equipment you carried in your hands, and acquired four laser derringers. This will contribute to the mission's success."

"There are many German citizens who want their country returned to a democracy and the hatred and killing stopped."

"Tonight, you must sleep. You won't remember my thoughts when you wake up in the morning."

"However, your subconscious will prevent you from disclosing information that should not be revealed. Like time travel."

"I have suggested to you, while you've been asleep during your stay at the safe house, that you cannot reveal anything about time travel. Your team members accept your enhanced strength and senses.

They know you can teleport and have electro-kinetic ability. That's all they can know."

"When an immortal travel forward in time, their future self is automatically removed to another dimension. Their body will be asleep and floating in midair. However, their mind is awake and experiencing all the sensations of the mission you are undertaking. They believe they're accomplishing the mission because they can see, hear, and feel everything going on. When the mission is over, and you return to 1688, they will return in a matter of seconds, believing they have completed the mission."

"Here are some rules to remember. The immortal must never reveal to others what they have discovered in the future. You cannot travel backwards in time from 1688. You can take objects forward in time, but you can't bring objects back from the future. Your twentieth century clothing would not exist. You would have to change back to your brown robe and emerald green pants, to avoid arriving naked. When 1944 arrives, you have an advantage. You may write down what you experienced from this mission on a scroll, then store it in a safe until that date. When the future you experienced arrives, it will be the present, and you can reveal what you wrote down on the scroll to others. This will help produce the best plans for the situation."

"Now enjoy a restful sleep and wake up well rested on a crispy sunny morning."

AUTHOR'S NOTE

Sally is a maturing immortal when she arrives in 1944. She will receive her special abilities in eight days. There doesn't seem to be a standard time for the immortal to reach maturity. Every individual immortal is different. Sometimes they receive the same super-ability and sometimes their super-ability is different. So far, we have ten superheroes heroes for Azorka and three superheroes for the Wizard's civilization.

Sally has accidentally traveled more than two-hundred-fifty years into the future. She held the silver crystal skull, from Indie's ancient globe, in such a way that it activated, shed its camouflage and turned gold. The crystal skull provides Sally's shape-shift inside a grey amoeba and her time travel to 1944.

Sally eventually learns the time travel rules for 'Immortals' and these rules must be followed while the crystal skull is able to control the time-lines for the good of the universe.

We learned in 'Adventure in Ancient Azorka-Immortal,' that Aleko moved more than four-thousand years into the future but came back and told mortals what he had learned. He was an immortal from the 'Yetz' solar system, and from the same planet the Wizard had been expelled from because of his rebel activities. As a counselor living in Village 'A', Aleko was trying to help Azorka win its struggle against the Wizard.

When Aleko came back to Azorka and warned of the 'Great Flood' and other facts he had learned from the future, he broke one of the time travel rules. He mysteriously disappeared shortly after this. Maybe he was sent back to his own planet, but we don't know.

Tonight, while in her sleep, the crystal skull has told Sally that she can't travel backwards in time. However, later in the series, we learn that the crystal skull can allow an immortal to travel backwards in time, out-of-body and view the past in order to adjust in their present time. But Sally would not be able to touch or communicate with anyone in that timeline. She'd be like a ghost.

All immortals understand that when a traveler moves forward in time, they will be removed and held in another dimension in a state of suspended animation. But their minds are living out the mission. They hear and see and feel the experience while in the dimension, with their bodies in a state of suspended animation. It is as though the crystal skull has given them a front row seat in the mind of the traveler. When the mission is complete, they return from this dimension, and carry on with their life unaware that they have been replaced. The same immortal will have the same crystal skull and may be called upon for a mission, which they know will cause the displacement of their future self.

The crystal skull is also a watcher possessing an unusual ability that allows it to remotely view the future and act when learning that intervention is necessary. It can also view the thoughts of others and see through solid objects in order to learn the directions necessary to guide the traveler to a location.

Objects taken forward in time is permitted. Bringing an object back from the future is impossible, as it hasn't been produced or invented yet. It is unknown as to how changes are made in present time, and show up instantaneously in future time.

The crystal skull, the watcher and provider of time travel, never explains why the mission is necessary. Perhaps the crystal skull is protecting someone in the future by preventing a disaster. We might never know in the future stories to come, but Sally appreciates any help they might get to oppose the Wizard's plans.

www.ingramcontent.com/pod-product-compliance
Lightning Source LLC
Chambersburg PA
CBHW071430300726
48976CB00004B/1290